The Solstice Conspiracy

A Novel for Young Readers

Lee Rawn

Lightspeed Publishing LLC
Arlington, Vermont

October 2010

v1.0

To my parents, Bob and Anne, and my children,
Craig and Beth

Table of Contents

Acknowledgements

Thank you to Lee Purcell for publishing guidance, editor Mary Johnson for exceptional wordsmithing throughout, and Les Ellenor for his helpful early read-through.

Chapter One

The Rat Hole

Doors flew open, and two children scrambled from the car. For the first time, Beth and Chris saw their new home. Icicles clung to the eaves. Once gleaming tusks, they had melted to a dog-toothed grin. Ice glossed the porch in the cold morning air. The house stood silent.

They ran up the walk and onto the porch, where the ice crackled under their feet. Eager to catch a glimpse inside, the children pressed against the window, but the house revealed only shadow.

"Let's go in." Chris tugged at Beth's arm.

"Hold on a minute." Their mother followed more cautiously. She pulled a key from her pocket and unlocked the door. "We'll wait for your father."

Beth and Chris watched with impatience while their dad maneuvered a rented moving truck into the driveway. Stepping down from the truck, he crunched across the frosty lawn, joining them on the porch.

"I'm first," Chris said, muscling his way to the front.

"No way." Beth grabbed his sleeve.

Chris's hand shot out, seized the doorknob and gave it a twist. With elbows, shoulders, and laughter, they spilled over the threshold and stopped. The laughter vanished and they gaped in surprise. Darkness filled every corner. The musty air hung thickly.

"It's been empty for a few years," their mother said, reaching for a light switch. Bare bulbs cast a dingy light, doing little to dispel the gloom.

"It looks bad now," their father said, "but with renovations, you'll see a big difference."

Beth and Chris exchanged a look.

"It means work," their father said, reading their thoughts, "and we're counting on you to help."

"Where do we sleep?" Chris asked.

"In the two bedrooms upstairs."

Chris took off up the wide staircase, with Beth close behind. Each wanted the best room. Peeling wallpaper greeted them and dust coated the floor. A broken window had been patched with cardboard and duct tape.

"What a dump," Chris said.

"Do they expect us to sleep here?" Beth frowned, and moved in for a closer look at the window "What are those?" Tiny black cylinders peppered the sill. "Are they dead bugs?"

"No, we have mice."

She pictured hoards of rodents running over her bed while she slept. "I think I'll take the other room."

"Beth, if there are mice in this room, you'll find mice in the other."

The smaller bedroom showed no improvement. Grime covered hideous pink walls, and scars gouged the floor.

"I've decided to take the big room," Beth said.

"Me too."

"Come on, Chris, I need the big room for all my stuff." She turned and walked back down the hall, intending to stake her claim.

"I'm taking the big room," he said, following her. "I should have it. I'm the oldest."

Beth was eleven, and two years younger than her brother. She whipped around to face him. "What's that got to do with anything?" By the set of his mouth, she could see that Chris was determined. "Fine, I'll look at the other room again." She headed back to the small bedroom, annoyed at Chris, but mostly at herself for backing down.

The walls will be painted, she thought, looking at the room with a critical eye. *I could cover the floor with a rug. But why should I get the small room?* She opened the closet door expecting to find a cramped little space. Instead, she found a sizeable attic. *That's why. This can be my reading room,* she thought, stepping inside.

Something smelled. Beth covered her nose, and then moving her hand away, took a tentative sniff. The air held a pungent musky odor, reminding her of cages at a zoo. *More rodents?* The thought sent a shiver. She cast about for signs of mice, but the floor was bare.

Daylight filtered down through a small window set high along the roofline, showing her the immediate area. It was a room large enough to convert into her own private haven. The rest of the attic tunneled off into a dim corridor. She guessed it ran the full length of the house and decided to explore that part of the attic later.

The thought of fixing up the attic outweighed her misgivings about the smell. *And anyway, hot soapy water should do the trick.* Looking around the room, she mentally arranged her furniture. A cozy chair, reading lamp, and bookshelves—all would fit easily into the space.

Light bloomed along the ceiling, illuminating the shadowed attic. The window glowed with sunlight, which didn't seem possible. At this time of day, sunshine fell upon the east side of the house. *What is that?* Beth tilted her head back and watched the play of light bounce among the rafters. After a moment the light faded and the attic reclaimed its customary gloom.

She waited to see if the light would come back, but nothing happened. Returning to the bedroom, Beth walked to the window. She used the arm of her sweater to rub away some of the grime, and peered through. Her jaw dropped.

Several acres stretched down a long slope, littered with tires, car parts, and other refuse. A stand of birches and some shrubs were the only evidence of nature. With a sinking heart she took in the debris. The cleanup would be monumental. Her gaze swept down the hill, coming to rest on the birches. They stood tall and leafless, silver sentinels in bright contrast to the dilapidation.

Despite leaving the home they had always known, the move from an apartment to their own house had been exciting. *But not here,* she thought, *it's a rat hole.*

"Did you make up your mind, Beth?" Chris came up behind her.

"Take the big room, Chris, I really don't care," she said, still looking out the window.

"What's the matter?" He asked, stepping up to the glass. "Oh no, the yard is as bad as the house."

"You got that? - 'Chris and Beth,'" Rill whispered over his shoulder.

"I got it." Leaning in the deeper shadows of the attic, Strega pushed himself away from the wall. "Move over," he said, "let me take a look." The attic door stood ajar, and Strega edged into position for a clear view.

"Humans, eh," Rill spoke into his ear, "throwing their names around without any caution whatsoever. That makes our job easier."

"Keep it down. There's something about that one." Strega lifted his chin toward Beth. "She saw that pathetic light with no trouble. I don't want to chance her spotting us." He pulled back from the door. "We'll wait for them to leave."

"When we go," Rill said, "let's snag the parents' names. It shouldn't be too hard."

The door swung wide and two lanky figures slipped through. The faintest of shadows, only the disturbance of air hinted at their presence. Long limbs floated, skimming above the floor's surface, pausing at the top of the stairs. Feral eyes scanned the floor below. They listened with interest, and before long, collected their final information, "Steve and Anne." Satisfied, they left unseen, mantled in shadow.

Chapter Two

Captured by Light

"Can you believe how excited Mom and Dad are?" Beth whispered to Chris. They both picked up a box from the truck and walked back to the house, following behind their parents.

"No, I can't. They haven't stopped smiling all morning."

"Wait and see how long that lasts." Beth shifted the box for a better grip.

They unloaded the truck through the morning, and part of the afternoon. Later, grateful for a break, Beth rested on her bed among the clutter of boxes and furniture piled high.

Light flickered across the ceiling. *There it is again.* She pushed herself off the bed and from the window saw a shimmer of light coming from the birches. It grew stronger as she watched. A soft ringing followed, quickly rising to an uncomfortable pitch. Clamping her hands over her ears, she attempted to block the sound. The ringing intensified, vibrating loudly inside her head. *What's happening to me?*

The light expanded with astonishing brilliance, and yet, she could look into the glow without shielding her eyes. It tugged at the edges of her mind, growing more insistent, until she surrendered to its pull. Golden warmth tingled through her body, and her heart fluttered against her chest.

Caught in the wonder of the moment, Beth was unprepared when an intense wave of grief issued from the light. It flooded through her, replacing warmth with sorrow. Her breath caught in her throat, and she struggled to pull away.

A second wave descended, more powerful than the first. The grief was familiar, not unlike how she had felt when her grandmother had died. Beth had visited her in the hospital, but her grandmother didn't recognize her. Although Beth knew it wasn't her grandmother's fault, she had felt deeply hurt.

Now, as then, the sorrow was more than she could bear, and closing her eyes, she wept. She cried for the nameless grief. She cried for her grandmother. She cried for herself.

Beth lost all sense of time. Eventually, the light softened, easing its grip. The sorrow was gone, and in its place grew a sense of relief. Without question, she knew that her tears had washed grief from the light.

But, what was that? Was it good, bad? She tried to make sense of what had happened. The light had not tried to hurt her, of that she was certain. She squinted into the glow, hoping to see more, hoping to find an explanation.

"Beth." The sound of her name intruded her thoughts.

Chris gave a tap on the open door. "Didn't you hear me calling? Dad has to take the truck back. We'll follow in the car and then stop for pizza. Come on."

She turned from the window, her face streaked with tears.

"What's wrong?"

"There's this light in the birches," her voice shook. "Something happened."

"Does this have to do with moving? Because if it does, it's hard on me too you know."

"It's not about the move." Beth looked back out the window, but the light was gone.

Chris looked over her shoulder. "I don't see a light."

"It isn't there anymore."

"What's going on?"

"If I tell you, you have to take this seriously."

Chris hid a smile. "Absolutely seriously."

"There was a brilliant light, and it had feelings, very strong feelings."

"You're kidding, right?"

"No, and I can prove it too." Actually, Beth wasn't certain that she could prove it, but she had to try. The experience had left her confused and unsettled. She needed Chris to believe her.

"The light is possible," Chris said, lending minimal support, "but the feelings were yours."

"I know. I felt sad, but it wasn't really me. It's too hard to explain. Just come with me, and I'll show you."

"Be right back," Chris called to his parents, following Beth out the door.

She pointed, from the top of the hill. "There, the light came from those trees."

"Let's take a look." Chris said.

They walked down the long slope avoiding the last patches of snow. The afternoon had brought warmer temperatures to hasten the thaw. Hints of life sprung from around the rubbish. Snowdrops, the first flower of the year to bloom, were unfolding tiny petals at the borders of the retreating snow. Beth's spirits lifted when she saw them.

A loose tendril of brown hair ribboned across her cheek, and she tucked it behind her ear. With dark wavy hair and hazel eyes, Beth's looks favored those of her father. Chris took after his mother, fair with blue eyes.

Following Chris down the hill, she noticed how much taller he had become, seemingly overnight. Beth remained short. She wondered if she was due for a growing spurt and hoped it would come soon. And when would her voice mature? To her own ears, she sounded like she had just started kindergarten.

Beth wasn't a little kid anymore. She wasn't a big kid either, but she could feel herself changing. Eleven years old seemed very different than ten. She knew that her love of reading had played a part in the changes she now felt. It was the knowledge she had gained from books, that helped propel her toward big kid status. That bit of extra knowledge also gave her a boost on the confidence meter.

"The light could be anything," Chris said, waiting while she caught up. "I bet we'll find broken glass or maybe a piece of metal reflecting the sun." He pointed to a shimmer in the trees. "Right there."

Beth frowned. "No, I don't think so. The light I saw was very bright." A sense of sadness settled around them, faint, but unmistakable. "Wait, there it is. Do you feel sad?" she asked.

Chris said nothing.

"Can you feel some sadness?"

"You know I feel sad," he said, with irritation. "I left my friends behind, just like you." He refused to buy into Beth's story of "feeling lights." However, the suddenness at which the sadness had appeared did seem odd.

As they drew near, the light brightened for an instant, and then winked out. Chris rooted around the trees. "Here's your light," he said, relieved to find an explanation. A chrome car bumper reflected a dull shine in the sun.

Beth looked down at the bumper, one more piece of refuse among many. "This is a car bumper. Car bumpers aren't usually sad."

Chris waved a dismissive hand. "The mystery is solved."

Chaper Three

Endangered Species

Get up." Thornby burst from the winter grass, skidding to a stop before his friend. "Call a meeting. Organize a work crew."

Artemus lounged in a discarded sardine can. The rolled tin lid served nicely as a pillow. "You're blocking the sun." He motioned for Thornby to step aside.

Thornby stood his ground, eyeing Artemus with distaste. "You're greasy, you're lazy, and you smell like rotten fish."

"Relax," Artemus drawled. His hair lay flat, slicked against his head with a greasy sheen. "Oil baths are therapeutic. Good for the skin. Why don't you give it a try?"

"Aren't you rushing spring? The sun may be shining, but it's not very warm."

"It suits me fine. If you would like, you can have the bath when I've finished."

"I'll pass. Besides, there's no time for that. New people have moved into the house."

"I'm aware of that," Artemus said, "but it's no good. We've been through this before."

"This time will be different. I can feel it." Thornby sat down on the edge of the tin. "Don't you miss the old days, Artemus?"

"Of course. I'm making the best of a bad situation. You know how it works. When the garden runs down, we run down too right along with it."

"I can't stand what we've become," Thornby said.

"Face it, we're an endangered species. Now if you'll excuse me, I've more bathing to attend to." Artemus rolled on his side, and Thornby leapt to his feet, avoiding a stinking wave of fish oil.

He took another stab. "This is our chance to turn things

around."

Artemus would have none of it.

"Fine then, I'll handle things myself."

"Don't you be bothering with humans, Thornby. They will lead to trouble."

Chapter Four

A Tough Pygmy

W ho's the pip squeak?" Evelyn Chainy slouched at her
desk. Her long legs stretched into the aisle, as if she
owned the place.

"It's the new kid," Rosemary said.

"Rosemary DelVeccio, would you please face the front." Mrs.
Silver waited a moment while the class settled in. "Everyone, we
have a new student. Please welcome Beth Brinson."

A murmur of hellos greeted her.

That wasn't too bad, Beth thought, looking at the new faces.
But then, the faces looked back at her. Prickly heat crawled up her
neck, and her cheeks bloomed crimson. A chuckle rippled through
the class deepening her blush. She never liked being the center of
attention.

"You may take the empty desk by the window," Mrs. Silver said.

What a pain joining a class this late in the year, Beth thought.
Why couldn't we have moved in the summer?

After a dull morning of math and social studies, a bell signaled
lunch and the room cleared with fire-drill speed. There would be
no eating in the cafeteria today. The unusually warm weather lured
everyone outside.

Not a vacant bench could be found. Students swarmed
everywhere. Beth crossed to the far end of the school grounds and
perched on a stone -wall. Fishing through her pack, she pulled out
and opened a thermos of soup. *Still hot,* she thought, as the liquid
released a wisp of steam.

Observing the activity around her, she watched students in
twos and threes mill about, chatting and waving to one another.
One group of kids stood in a cluster, heads together in some secret
discussion.

It always took awhile for Beth to warm up to people. She

thought about the friends she had left behind—good friends—and wondered if she would ever see them again. Spotting Chris talking to a group of boys, she felt a stab of envy. He never had trouble fitting in.

The bell rang announcing the return to class, and she fell into step with the other students, trailing behind a group of girls. They were talking loudly and all at the same time. From the center of the group, a missile of candy wrapper launched over their heads, landing at Beth's feet.

Already fed up with the trash in her own yard, the candy wrapper irritated her. *How lazy is that?* She thought, retrieving the wrapper and dropping it into a nearby trashcan.

Someone nudged the tall girl and pointed to Beth. Evelyn Chainy whipped around.

"Who do you think you are, my mother?"

"The trashcan is right here," Beth said.

"I dropped it. And anyway, it's none of your business."

The girls laughed and waited to see what Beth would do.

For the second time that day, her cheeks flamed, but this time from anger. She balled her fists and glared at the girls.

"Aren't you the tough little pygmy." Evelyn took a menacing step closer.

Beth took a step back. Choosing the only sensible option, she turned away, and walked back to the school. A chorus of laughter followed.

Chris waited for her at the school entrance. "Way to make friends. You've been here half a day and already someone's mad at you."

"That's her problem."

"You know that saying 'pick on someone your own size'? You ought to think about that."

Chapter Five

Humor the Kid

The business of settling in continued. With her father's help, Beth painted her bedroom a soft sage green. Now that her furniture was in place, her room looked inviting.

Turning to the attic, she scrubbed the walls and floor. When the floor was dry, she positioned a comfortable chair below the window. Setting her bookshelf beside the chair, she unpacked her favorite books. Among them were old volumes, traditional tales of adventure and magic, which had belonged to her grandmother Margaret. *A light with feelings is magic too*, she thought, *and it happened in the real world.*

Beth walked down to the birches several times during the week, hoping to see the light again, but without success. Nothing could be found to prove that the light had ever existed.

Rain tapered to a drizzle. *Doesn't it just figure*, Beth thought, squelching through the sodden grass, *after a week of sunshine, it rains on Saturday.* Clouds covered the sky with a leaden cast, promising another downpour.

It had been decided that Beth and Chris would be in charge of yard cleanup, while their parents tackled repairs on the house.

"If it starts raining again, I'm quitting," she said.

"Then let's get started." Chris grabbed a garbage bag. "I don't want this yard to eat up all my Saturdays. We'll start with the small stuff."

The rain held off and they worked steadily for a few hours.

"It's rotten luck having to clean the yard," Chris said, stuffing trash into a bag.

"I'd rather clean the yard than sand floors." Beth dragged a heavy bag struggling over some rough ground. A piece of glass cut through the plastic.

"Good point, but look at the size of this yard. It's a huge job. And what are we supposed to do with all the big stuff, like that old truck?"

An abandoned truck poked through a clump of bushes. The hood was missing, and a small tree twisted around the motor in an effort to reach sunlight.

"Mom and Dad will probably hire someone to tow it away," Beth said. With effort, she hoisted her bag onto the growing pile behind the garage.

Satisfied with their progress, they sat on an old potting bench to take a break. Beth looked over at Chris, struggling with an inner debate. Sometimes he could be hard to talk to, but she just couldn't let her thought go.

"What?" he asked, feeling her eyes upon him.

"I think the light we saw was magical."

"Don't start with the light again."

"It wasn't just a light, and I know you felt something."

Chris shrugged. "All right, I did notice something, but that doesn't lead me to magic."

"You think a car bumper with feelings makes sense?"

Chris threw her a "humor the little kid" look and stood. "Let's do a little more and then pack it in."

They wandered farther down the slope, stopping by a flat truck tire on a rusted rim. Rolling it up the hill proved more difficult than expected. Wet grass and decaying leaves were slick from the rain, causing them to slip and slide.

Chris set the tire on its side and knelt on the ground. "There's something here." Digging into the dead grass, he seized a clump of sod and tugged. It lifted easily, revealing a stone step.

Beth leaned forward and reached for the next step, feeling its hardness beneath the grass. Gradually, with fingers scraped and caked with dirt, they unearthed seven stone steps.

"These stairs were built a long time ago. The mortar between the stones is crumbling badly," Chris said, crushing a chunk between his fingers. He looked at Beth and seeing disappointment, started to laugh. "Were you expecting a fairy mound or a secret door?"

"Well, no, but wouldn't it be great?"

"You read too many stories," he said. "The stairs are probably part of a rock garden." He stood up. "Let's quit and get some lunch. I'm starving."

"I see you've found the old rock stairs," said a voice.

Startled, the children spun around to see who could have spoken. Peering over the hedge from the neighboring yard stood a very small woman wearing a very large hat. The brim veiled her eyes, but the children could feel her gazing intently. She had a round weathered face and an easy smile. "Please, come over," she called, waving.

As they drew near, Chris muttered, "She's not much taller than you. I'll bet she's the fairy queen."

"Cut it out, Chris."

"I've been looking forward to meeting you," the woman said. "It's good to have neighbors again. My name is Mrs. Peasgood," she said with a nod.

"I'm Chris, and this is my sister, Beth."

Usually Beth felt shy around new people, but Mrs. Peasgood had an enchanting smile. Beth found herself unexpectedly at ease in her presence.

"I'm delighted to see you working in the yard. Did you know that at one time, this yard had many gardens and lawns? The flowers were so exceptional that people traveled from great distances to admire them."

"You wouldn't know that to look at it now," Chris said. "What happened?"

"I'm just about to go in for lunch. Why don't you join me for tea and sandwiches, and I'll tell you about the garden."

"That sounds good," Chris nodded. "What do you think, Beth?"

"Okay, but we'll need a few minutes to wash up." She held up her dirt encrusted hands.

You might want to check with your parents. They may already

have lunch waiting for you. Let me know if you can't come. Otherwise, I'll see you shortly."

Beth burst into the kitchen. "Mom, Dad, we've just met the lady next door. She is very nice and has invited us over for lunch."

"We met Mrs. Peasgood a few days ago while you were at school," their mother said. "I think you'll enjoy your visit. She is a very interesting person."

Chapter Six

A Secret Revealed

Should I ask about the light?"

"Do yourself a favor and don't," Chris said, as they approached Mrs. Peasgood's house.

"She might know something."

"Just ask about the garden."

Mrs. Peasgood's house stood back from the road, screened by a thick row of cedars.

"Just in time," she greeted them. "Everything is ready."

Inside, the house was bright and cheery. They walked to the kitchen, stopping once to admire a painting of colorful flowers, that had been signed "E. Peasgood."

A large platter of sandwiches awaited them, and the steaming pot of tea smelled like mint.

"Please, sit down and help yourselves," Mrs. Peasgood said, pulling a chair up to the table.

"Good sandwich," Beth said. It was peanut butter and strawberry jam, and Beth was sure the jam was homemade. "Have you lived here very long?" she asked between bites.

"For many years."

"Does anyone else live here?" Chris asked.

"Just me. Mr. Peasgood passed away some time ago, and my children have homes of their own. They visit, though, bringing lots of grandchildren. At other times, I'm a bit of a hermit."

"What do you do when you are by yourself?" Beth asked. She mopped up a spot of jam with a piece of crust.

"I like to garden."

"What about in the winter?"

"I enjoy painting. Most of my days are full. It's a balance between the chaos of a full house and solitude."

When they finished their sandwiches and sipped a second cup of tea, Chris asked about the garden. "How did it go from garden to junkyard?"

Mrs. Peasgood looked at them steadily. "Yes, I suppose we should discuss the garden. As I've told you, it used to be beautiful, but there is more to it than that." She paused for a moment, and then seemed to come to a decision. "To say anything further," she said, "I would have to reveal a secret. Could I count on you to keep it to yourselves?"

Beth and Chris looked at each other, and then nodded.

"We promise," Beth said, leaning in to catch every word.

"Good. The garden hiding beneath the rubbish is no ordinary garden." She looked at them in all seriousness. "It has feelings."

Beth sat up straight, turning to Chris with a satisfied smile.

"When you say 'feelings,'" he said, ignoring his sister, "what exactly do you mean?"

"When the garden was cared for, the air filled with fragrance, and like scent carried on a breeze, one could detect a hint of feeling."

"Was it sad?" Beth asked.

"No, happy, usually, but sometimes it grew to overwhelming joy. Not everyone could sense this. However, all who visited the garden left with a feeling of well-being and a smile on their lips."

"Last week, I saw a light coming from the birches," Beth confided, "and it was very sad."

"Did you indeed," Mrs. Peasgood said, "This is interesting news."

"Later that day, Chris and I both saw it, but the light wasn't as strong."

Mrs. Peasgood looked at Chris.

Good going, Beth, involve me, he thought, fidgeting with his napkin. "I did notice something," he said.

"You're not comfortable with this, are you Chris." Mrs. Peasgood said.

"No, not really."

"Two people can see the same thing and come away with a different explanation." She poured the last few drops of tea into their cups and smiled. "It's not a question of who is right, but having the 'right' to your own opinion. Each opinion has its value."

Chris returned her smile, feeling easier.

"It's differences that make the world interesting." Mrs. Peasgood said, pushing away from the table. "Excuse me for a moment." She walked to the cupboard, and with the aid of a stepping stool, pulled down a plate of cookies. "Ginger," she said, and passed them around.

"What happened to the garden?" Beth asked.

"A long time ago, a couple moved in next door. They had no children, and most of their time was devoted to gardening. Both had great imaginations for designing flower beds and rock gardens."

"I think we found one of the rock gardens today," Chris said.

"Yes, by the stone steps," Mrs. Peasgood said. "What made the garden unique was not the design or variety of flowers, but the way it was looked after. The plants were lovingly cared for, as if each flower was a tiny child. The garden flourished."

Chris bit into a second cookie. They were good, crisp on the outside, chewy in the middle, with just the right amount of ginger burn.

"As the couple grew older, they were not able to care for the garden as they once had." Mrs. Peasgood said, pausing for a sip of tea. "They let parts of it grow wild, which was all right. Unrestrained, a deeper beauty emerged."

"Where did all the junk come from?" Chris asked. He found it difficult to imagine the garden as Mrs. Peasgood described, especially having spent the morning filling garbage bags.

"They died, and not having any children, the house and land went to a cousin. He was a nice enough young man, but had a compulsive need to collect things—especially things mechanical. His dream was to rebuild old cars and sell them. He tinkered a bit in the garage, but never completed any projects. Perhaps he couldn't find all the necessary parts. I don't know."

"Having no interest in plants, he saw the garden as a convenient area for storage. Soon old car parts and bits of garbage littered the ground. The garden declined rapidly. For a while, one could sense sadness, and then nothing."

"That must have been a while back," Beth said, "because the house is falling apart too."

"He put the place up for sale about eight years ago. When it didn't sell right away, he moved out. The house has remained empty all this time."

"Mom and Dad are excited to have their own house," Beth said. "They plan to renovate the whole thing."

"I'm glad you and your parents are here. The place looks better already."

They spoke of many things that afternoon. What Beth enjoyed most, was how genuinely interested Mrs. Peasgood was with what she and Chris had to say.

A gust of wind caused a branch to scratch and squeak at the kitchen window. The children looked out at the darkening sky with surprise. The afternoon had gone by quickly.

"We should get going," Chris said. "Thank you for lunch."

"Yes, thank you," Beth said, rising from her chair.

Mrs. Peasgood showed them to the door. "I have no explanation for your experience with the light," she said, "but I would take it as a sign of good things to come. Perhaps your young energy will pull the garden back to health."

The wind tugged at their jackets, and they quickened their pace toward home.

"I like her," Beth said.

"Me too."

"After we clear out the junk, I'm going to be a gardener."

"You don't know the first thing about gardening," Chris said.

"That's okay. I'll read up on it and just try a little here and there. Do you want to give it a try?"

"I'll think about it."

Arriving at home, they took the porch steps two at a time.

Chapter Seven

The Devious Plan

From a sheltered tussock of grass, Thornby studied the children with interest. All morning, they filled bag after bag with garbage and hauled it away.

His heart quickened when they knelt on the hillside. *What drew them there?* he wondered, watching them unearth the first step. An important gathering place, the old stone steps had remained unused and buried for years.

Memories swelled his heart, as he remembered days of music and dance, learning, and celebration. Known as one of the great cultural centers, folks had traveled from the farthest realms to partake in the yearly festivals.

Shame intruded his thoughts. His people were entrusted with the care of this land, yet little remained of its greatness. Sure, there was an occasional local festival, but the great gatherings had ended.

A plan began to form in his head, rapidly taking shape. It was bold, but he ignored rising doubts and squared his shoulders. *Someone has to do this*, he thought, *and it falls to me.*

His encounter with Artemus came to mind. All the fairies were mired in laziness. Thornby, himself, often felt too tired to budge, but he clung to the thought of better times, and this helped him get going. *I'll need an ally,* he thought.

Juniper lived on the outskirts of the fairy settlement at Firefly Hollow. Because of the distance, Thornby thought she would be less affected by the lethargy gripping the garden dwellers. He remembered her as a plucky sort. *I'll start with her.*

Looking out of her cozy bower, Juniper saw Thornby striding up the path. One hand anchored his hat, the other clutched his cloak, which billowed in the March wind.

"Something must be important to bring you here on such a

windy day," she said. "Please come in." Taking his hat and cloak, she directed him to a chair. Instead of joining him, she disappeared into a pantry, returning with a plate of little cakes. They dripped with honey, and Thornby popped one into his mouth, savoring every sticky crumb.

He took a moment to look around. "Nice to see a home done up in the old style," he said, then reached for another piece of cake.

The dwelling was a traditional fairy bower. Juniper had built the bower herself, weaving living branches to spiral around one another, forming a wide tunnel. The tight weave created a snug shelter, free from wind and snow. In the summer, the branches wreathed her in dark green leaves and fragrant white flowers.

It wasn't often that Juniper had company, and she delighted in sharing cakes with Thornby. Also, a bit of news would be welcome.

"What brings you out here?" she asked.

"A family has moved into the house."

"How nice. Is that supposed to mean something?"

"It does mean something. It means that we have a chance to turn things around," Thornby said, more forcefully than he'd intended.

"And why do you think this time will be different?"

He told her about the children and the work they had done in the garden.

"Well, good," she said with an edge to her voice. "They don't like living in garbage either."

Thornby began to speak, but she cut him off. "Removing some garbage is a far cry from the help we need. They're human after all, not very reliable."

"There's more. I don't know if it means anything, but I saw a light in the birches—actually more of a glimmer. But what interested me was that the children saw it too. They even went to investigate."

"If the children saw a light, then they only saw some reflection. None of this is our concern." Juniper said.

"But what if it was the light?" Thornby persisted.

Juniper looked thoughtful. "What exactly are you asking of me?"

"I'm asking for change."

"We could certainly use a turnaround," she said. "I can feel the garden pulling me down. Sometimes, I can barely get up in the morning and that worries me. Not because of the children, but because we need change, I'll help."

Thornby breathed deeply, not realizing he had been holding his breath. "Thank you," he said.

"For change, we need the help of all the fairies," Juniper said, "and they won't do a thing to help themselves." She drummed her fingers on the table.

"We'll ask the children to help restore the garden," Thornby said.

"Put the children aside for a moment. First, we must rally the fairies. That is our biggest problem."

"We'll have to meet in a group," Thornby said, "but it's impossible."

Juniper smiled. "No, not impossible. What is the one thing a fairy can't resist?"

Thornby looked blank.

"A celebration. When did we last dance on Midsummer's Eve? The gatherings are always hosted by the elves, and that's a three-day walk from here. We should host the celebration this year. We'll send out invitations to everyone."

"What?" Thornby cried. "How can you suggest such a thing? Have you looked around? The garden is a shambles. Our people are a shambles."

Juniper laid a hand on Thornby's arm, ignoring his outburst. "Here's what I'm thinking. We send invitations to the elves and sprites for our midsummer celebration. We'll invite the fauns, of course; they're the best musicians. Now, here's the important part of the plan. Once our invitations have been sent, we'll let the local folks know of the upcoming event, and tell them we'll need their help with the preparations."

"That's it? That's your plan? They'll be furious."

"Exactly. This will really shake them up." Juniper laughed. "They'll have to call a meeting to straighten out the problem that we created."

"You devious little fairy. I'll bet impish blood runs in your family."

Chapter Eight

Bedtime Ritual

The "Future Beth" essay was causing anxiety. Beth had always worked hard in school and made good grades. So when her essay came back marked with a "C" she chafed at the unfair assessment. The scrawl of red ink jumped off the page: "Lack of research. No sense of commitment."

"I decided not to be a marine biologist," Beth had said, when her mother looked up from the essay. "So when I got the assignment, I didn't know what to write about."

"You were caught between jobs," her mother said, smiling. "Don't worry. I still have no idea what to be when I grow up." When Beth didn't return her smile, she added, "Something will present itself at the right time."

And something had. One afternoon with Mrs. Peasgood, and "What to be" fell into place. She would be a gardener—or maybe a landscaper. Ideas crowded her mind: visions of garden paths flanked in color, shrubs loaded with blooms, berry bushes, and trees. Just having the ideas made her feel as if she had already started. Her new home took on a different light. The house and yard, despite their condition, opened all kinds of possibilities. Beth and her family could pretty much do anything.

Beth turned down the bed. It had been a full day. She closed the attic door and switched on the nightlight. A small bulb illuminated a disc of mauve and blue stained glass. She'd had the nightlight since she was a baby. When all the other lights were out, the soft glow transformed her room into something otherworldly. It transported her to a castle chamber, lit by moonlight. Sometimes she fancied herself camping in the desert under a canopy of stars. *Tonight it's the desert*, she thought, and soon dropped off.

Creaking hinges pulled Beth from sleep. She flipped over on her side and watched the attic door swing wide. *How did that happen? Is the latch broken?*

Open closet doors are not acceptable at bedtime. This rule was made a long time ago, when monsters lived in closets and under the bed. Now that she was older, she continued to close the closet door out of habit. Other rules, such as "safety zones" had long been discarded. The safest zone had been under the covers, provided all limbs were completely tucked in. Allowances were made for fresh air and only her nose had periscoped above the blankets.

"Islands" offered safe passage to the bathroom. These, consisting of towels, quilts, and odd bits of clothing, covered the floor at intervals. The danger lay in the quality of the island. If it was a piece of clothing, it could slide when she jumped, forcing her to step off.

All manner of creatures hovered nearby, ready to strike. The hall and bathroom were off limits to monsters, but the return to her bed was even more treacherous. They knew she would be coming back, and lurked around the islands ready to bite and claw. Beth smiled, thinking of her nightly rituals. When had she quit doing that?

Sleep tugged, but the gaping door bothered her. She should just get up and close it. Instead, by instinct and habit, she burrowed under the blankets closing her eyes. Moments later, her eyes popped open and she blew out a frustrated breath.

This is silly. Throwing off the covers, she got out of bed . . . and froze.

Yellow eyes blazed, floating in mid-air between Beth and the door. With a shriek, she bolted onto the bed and pressed against the wall.

"And now it begins," came a voice.

Beth screamed.

Chapter Nine

A Gift of Terror

Feet sounded from all over the house. Her parents pelted up the stairs and burst into her room, Chris right on their heels.

"What is it? What's wrong?" Her mother rushed to her side, wrapping her arms around Beth.

Lifting a shaking finger, Beth pointed.

"There's nothing there," her mother assured her. "It's okay, honey, you're having a bad dream."

"That's right, 'Beth,'" the voice said. "You're having a bad dream."

"There." Beth's voice rasped, and she started to cry.

Strega pulled his face close to her ear. A cloying odor, rank and rotting, caught in her throat and she gagged.

"Is she having a seizure?" her mother cried.

"I don't think so." Her father held her face in his hands. "Beth, look at me. You are having a nightmare."

"No one is there, Beth. Wake up," Chris said with an impatient edge.

"They don't see us, 'Beth,'" Strega said. His fetid breath stirred her hair, and she recoiled from his closeness. "Only you have the gift."

Another voice joined in. "Yes, think of us as gifts. Surprise!"

Strega lowered his voice, each word spoken clearly, emphatically. "You will bring us fully into this world."

Beth became quiet, her body rigid, as she absorbed his words.

"Don't stop crying. Crying is good—and screaming is downright delicious." Strega reveled in the control he had over Beth. "Fear and anger are the very things that make us whole," he boasted. "See? Solid." He flexed his fingers and poked Beth's arm.

She jerked away. "But it doesn't matter, solid or vapor, you will make us permanent and open the door for others."

He's going too far, bragging like that, Rill thought. Signaling to Strega, he melted back into the darkness.

"You're mine." Strega kissed her cheek.

A shudder ran through her body, and the tears began again.

"You are sleeping with us." Her father hoisted her in his arms.

Later, sandwiched between her parents, Beth felt safe. Overcome with exhaustion, she fell into a dreamless sleep.

She woke well into the afternoon, stiff and groggy. First the voice came back to her, followed by the smell. Her skin crawled at the thought of his touch.

Her mother peeked in the door. "You're up. That was quite a nightmare you had."

Beth wanted it to be a nightmare. She told herself that it was a nightmare, but her deeper self disagreed.

Everything looks the same, Beth thought, checking the bedroom. Setting a cup of water on the nightstand, she turned down the bed, switched on the nightlight and made sure the attic door was tightly closed. Not enough. Anxiety dictated that she change her routine. With some effort, she pushed her dresser in front of the attic door. She would keep her bedroom door open with the hall light turned on.

From her bed, she continued to examine the shadows, always coming back to the attic door. As the night wore on, sleep found her, and in the morning she was flooded with relief. Nothing had happened. This was true the next night and it continued to be so. Gradually, she felt more like herself. The door to the hall stood open a little less, until only a blade of light fell across the floor.

Beth started to think of her experience as a dream—a terrible dream that had continued with her eyes opened. *Not so different than a light taking over my body,* she decided. A light full of grief, a garden with feelings, a night of terror, these events were far from ordinary, and spoke of magic, good and bad. It should be thrilling that magic existed, but Beth felt alone.

Chapter Ten

The Turning Point

Groups of fairies headed for the stone steps. For fairies, they were not very quiet. Some grumbled, some complained loudly, and others looked cross. The air hummed like a beehive stirred with a stick.

"Juniper, what have we done?" Thornby asked, fighting the urge to run.

"We have done exactly what we set out to do." Juniper sounded more confident than she felt. "Let's go in. The meeting will be starting soon."

A stone at the top of the stairs had been rolled away, revealing the opening to the ancient hall.

"Just stick to the plan," Juniper said, stepping through.

The hall had not suffered from disuse. Someone had washed the floor and removed the dust. A woven carpet covered the speaker's platform. High along the walls, baskets lined with clay lit the hall with the soft glow of firefly milk.

Collecting this light was a responsibility the fairies never shirked, even in their present state of lethargy. By mutual need, fireflies were "milked" once a year.

Jostling one another in the packed hall, the fairies tried to find seats with a good view of the front. Elected officials, the council, watched from the speaker's platform, waiting for all to find their places.

Thornby and Juniper stood at the back amidst a deafening clamor. Everyone talked at once.

Vali, the chief councilor, rose and the assembly dropped to expectant silence. "As many of you have heard," his clear voice filled the hall, "this year's Midsummer's Eve celebration is to be held in our community." An angry murmur rippled among the fairies, and

Vali raised his hand for silence.

"Without the benefit of discussion and vote, invitations were sent far and wide, announcing our plans to host the event. Obviously, this puts us in an embarrassing situation. Two members of our community, Thornby and Juniper, for reasons I cannot understand, invited the entire realm of Faerie to join us. I think now would be a good time for them to come forward and explain themselves."

All heads turned, watching Thornby and Juniper thread their way to the front. Seats were pushed back on the crowded platform to make room. They stepped forward and faced the crowd.

"We know that you are not happy with us right now," Juniper began.

The fairies exploded with shouts and jeers.

"Please," Thornby hollered to be heard over the uproar, "give us a chance to explain." After a moment or two, the fairies were ready to listen. "Go ahead, Juniper."

Knowing how angry everyone would be, Juniper had memorized her speech to help her stay on track. She cleared her throat. "We have reached the darkest time in our history. There is no doubt that, left unchecked, it will become darker still. The turning point is now. To continue as we have spells the end of our existence."

"What about the humans?" Someone interrupted. "It's their fault."

"That may be, but we must be responsible for ourselves. Thornby and I think we've found a way to bring back the garden. Very likely it won't be as it was, but it could be enough to lift us out of our predicament."

"Oh sure," someone laughed, "We could make flower containers out of garbage."

"Most of you know that people have moved into the house. We intend to ask them for help."

No one spoke. They all stared at Juniper in amazement. Then someone found his voice.

"You can't be serious."

Thornby spoke up. "Already the children have worked in the

garden. Some of you saw them haul garbage away. And they dug out our stone stairs."

"So what," Artemus called out from the crowd. "What difference does it make?"

"I have a good feeling about them," Thornby said.

"You expect us to take a huge leap because you have a good feeling?" Artemus shot back.

"No I don't." Thornby felt uneasy with what he was about to say. It could be true, but he was stretching the truth to win them over. "Something extraordinary has already happened," he said. "The garden has shown its heart to the children."

The crowd gasped in astonishment.

"I saw it myself the first day they arrived," he added, strengthening his claim.

The strained atmosphere evaporated upon hearing the news. Excited chatter erupted, and Thornby felt the sting of guilt. Had he misled them? Very likely so.

"This is wonderful news," Vali said. "We thought the spirit of the garden had departed. However, it does not address the immediate problem of the celebration. And working with humans sounds unsavory."

"The garden has accepted the children. Who are we to ignore that?" Thornby said.

"The celebration, Thornby, is in three months," Vali said. "There's not enough time."

"Which is why we must share the work with the children."

Vali thought for a moment, weighing all that he had heard. He turned to the council. "Do we proceed?" All gave their consent but one. "Very well. How will you approach the children? I strongly doubt that they could see or hear you."

"We approach now," Juniper cut in. "It's the perfect time while we are gathered. Together we have the strength for a 'sending.' We'll do it while the children sleep."

Some of the fairies looked doubtful.

"It's the easiest way." Juniper insisted. "We'll keep it simple, starting with a picture of the garden as it was. At another time we might send something more detailed. Hopefully, in time, we'll be able to speak directly. To begin, we'll show them the part of the garden where we held our celebration," she suggested. "Restoring the entire garden isn't possible in so short a time, even with our help. Thornby, will you lead the sending?"

Settling comfortably in their seats, the fairies closed their eyes. Thornby spoke softly. "Do you all have a clear picture in your minds of the garden where we danced? Keep that vision. Now, include the children. Let them walk barefoot on soft grass. Wash the sweet fragrance of flowers over them and dazzle them with the brightness of the flowers' many colors."

The fairies sat united in thought. The very air shimmered, and a strong sense of peace enveloped their hearts.

This is indeed the turning point, Thornby thought, *and the first step is well begun.*

The feeling of peace continued, and the fairies left the hall drifting homeward on silent fairy feet.

Maeve watched the night sky from her window. Elegant cracks traversed the length of the glass, catching beads of moonlight. She had, by far, the largest, most unusual home in the community.

Yawning widely, she walked to her bedroom. It had a special feature, a red metal door. She tapped the silver button at its center, and the door sprang open. The interior was dark and cozy. Velvety moss provided a soft bed, and leaning in the corner sat her most valued possession—a jagged triangle of reflecting glass. This produced a perfect image of Maeve.

She lay on the moss, but sleep would not come. Maeve was on edge. She was not happy about the sending and had voted against it. *Why would anyone want to return to the old ways,* she thought. *I'm happy now. Am I expected to give up all this? Live in some bush next to everyone else?* The old truck had provided years of comfortable living. *What of my privacy? What of my possessions?* Tiny fists clenched. *I won't stand for it.*

Chapter Eleven

Sharing Weird

Flowers of every hue displayed a vision of light and color. Beth caught her breath in wonder. She turned slowly, taking in the magnificent garden, each view more exquisite than the last. Soft grass cushioned her feet, and she wriggled her toes, savoring the texture.

Those trees look familiar, she thought, watching the lowering sun slip in among the birches. Before she could wonder about them, a breeze, heavy with the scent of flowers, swept all thought away.

Beth could not tell how long she stood, captivated by sight and scent. Here was a place where time had no hold.

Some movement drew her back. A silhouetted figure emerged from the trees, walking in her direction. *It's Chris*, she thought, recognizing his gait. She sat on the grass and waited.

"Beth, you're in my dream," he said.

"I guess this is a dream, but it's mine."

Chris sat down beside her and plucked a blade of grass. It dangled from his lips, and he chewed at the tiny root. "I can actually taste the flavor of the grass," he marveled. "Everything is so real."

"It looks like another unsettled day. Winds from the northeast . . . ," a voice boomed. Beth bolted upright in bed, her head swimming in fog, while the clock radio hammered out the news and weather. As she swung her legs over the side of the bed, a riot of colors flashed in her mind. *The dream*, she thought, and remembered clearly.

The walk to the bathroom held a dream-like quality, while images of the garden seemed real. In the bathroom, she studied her face in the mirror. The girl gazing back appeared the same, but her eyes held a faraway look.

Back in the hall, she waited while Chris stumbled toward her, looking dazed.

He stopped and gave her a quizzical look. "I had an amazing dream," he said.

"About a garden," she replied.

He gaped in astonishment. "This is too weird," he said, and disappeared into the bathroom.

She pulled on her clothes. *Weird, good word choice*, she thought. *It's been nothing but weird since we moved in here*. But one thing Beth realized, with a rush of happiness, was she now shared "weird" with someone else.

Chapter Twelve

Don't Call it Magic

Shifting images of flowers and trees, streamed across her mind.

"Beth, are you with us?"

"Whaaa?" Her head snapped up, jolted into the present. "Sorry, Mrs. Silver, what did you ask me?"

"Is there something of interest out the window?"

"No."

"Then perhaps you could come up here and solve this math problem."

She pushed back from her desk, an elbow sweeping its surface in the process. Books crashed to the floor, followed by a flutter of paper. Laughter erupted all around her.

The entire day passed in a fog. She just couldn't focus. Leaving class at the end of the day was a great relief.

Chris looked up, his hand emerging from the cookie jar with a sizeable stack. "Hi Beth, you want some?"

"What kind?"

"Chocolate chip."

"Perfect, I'll get some milk." Returning from the fridge with two brimming glasses, she plunked down at the table and reached for a cookie.

They sat for a while, quietly munching.

"Have you ever heard of anyone sharing a dream?" Chris asked, breaking the silence.

"No, and the dream was so real, as if we were really there."

"To me, it looked familiar, like I've been there before."

"Me too," Beth said. "Strange things keep happening, first the light and now the dream."

"I have to admit it. Something is definitely going on," Chris said.

"Now you know I'm not making this stuff up."

"The light appeared both times by the birches," Chris said, brushing crumbs off his shirt, "Why don't we walk down there and take another look?"

"I was there twice last week," Beth said. "We won't find anything."

"Just a quick look before it gets too dark." Chris was already reaching for his jacket.

"Need a closer look at that car bumper?" Beth teased.

"I'm not ruling that out."

"What are we looking for?" Beth asked, wandering in and out of the trees.

"Not sure." Something pushed at Chris's memory. *I've done this before*, he thought. *No, that's not it. I've been here before . . .* His thoughts played out in a string of guesses. With a flash he realized. "Those trees were in our dream."

"No they weren't."

"See, there's the path I was walking on. You were over there." He pointed. "Go on, stand there." He waved her away.

She stood on what might have been the spot and watched Chris walk toward her. "No, everything is different," she called out.

"Of course everything is different. Our dream was in the summertime."

"You're right, this is amazing," Beth said, her eyes lit with excitement. "The light, the dream, it's all magic."

Chris frowned and looked up at the sky. "We should get back before dark," he said, starting back up the hill at a fast clip.

Beth trotted after him. "So, that has to be the garden the way it was," she said, catching up, "like Mrs. Peasgood described." Ideas formed faster than she could process them, and she spoke in an excited rush.

Chris quickened his pace, leaving her behind.

"See you back at the house," he flung over his shoulder.

What's his problem? she thought, staring after him.

"Very effective," Rill said. Some of his transparency receded to solid form. "I can feel my hands, but it's not enough. Why didn't you hurl a sending at the girl? We could be eating solids tonight." He pictured a fat rodent in his bony fingers.

"Rill, you have a natural aptitude, but you lack experience. For the boy, 'magic' is the negative trigger. So, we heighten his feelings with a sending. For the girl, I have chosen the natural route." He gestured toward Beth. "There's confusion there and a big helping of hurt. Breathe it in, Rill." Strega took a deep breath and let it out. "Ah." His vaporous body gained more substance.

"Yes, it's good," Rill agreed, "but why not go in now and give them everything we've got?" He slammed his fist into his hand, savoring the sensation. "Come on, what do you say?"

"You would choose a temporary solution, foregoing the mission? What would we gain?"

"We would be whole."

"And why would we want that?"

Rill shot him a look. "Senses, Strega, especially taste." He spoke with emphasis, as if tutoring a young wiggin.

"True, but wholeness is nothing without permanency. This is but the first of many battles—a testing ground. Remember that we are honored emissaries. The wiggins chose us to clear the way for the first assault."

"Couldn't we push ahead just a little? Even if we were solid, we'd still be invisible."

"Not to her."

"I hope you know what you're doing."

"Who's the leader here?" Strega cuffed him on the head. "Ha, partial form does have its advantages," he grinned.

"I only meant that we might have left things too late." Rill rubbed the back of his head. "Who would have thought that those wretched fairies could band together for a sending?"

"No need to worry. They're weak. One lousy sending took the whole lot of them."

Beth walked slowly back to the house, and they watched her go. Strega rejoiced in his own cleverness. "You see? Without lifting a finger, she will bear the pain of her family turning against her one by one. Before long she'll feel so angry and hurt, we can seize her will. After that she'll happily do our bidding."

Chapter Thirteen

Betrayed

Dusk had turned to dark when Beth pushed through the kitchen door.

"There you are, Beth. How was school today?" her mother asked.

"Okay. How was your day at the store? Did the books arrive?"

"Not yet, but it's fine because we haven't finished putting up the shelves. It'll take at least another week before we open."

Her parents looked tired. Not only were they fixing up the house, they were also preparing to open a bookstore in town—something they had always wanted to do.

Everyone moved about the kitchen, congenially bumping into one another, as dinner pulled together. The food smelled wonderful, and Beth's stomach responded with a growl.

Part way through the meal, Beth put down her fork. "Mom, Dad, have you noticed anything unusual since moving in?"

Chris looked up from his plate, catching Beth's eye. He gave a small shake of his head.

"Unusual, how?" her father asked.

Beth looked at Chris and raised her chin defiantly. "Chris and I saw a mysterious light in the birches, and it was sad."

"Sad? How?" Her mother asked.

"It's hard to explain, but when we saw it, we both started to 'feel' sad. And then there was the dream."

Chris sat up straight, pursing his lips. "What dream was that, Beth?"

"You know, Chris. We both had the same dream about a garden."

"No we didn't. Don't be crazy."

"I'm not crazy." Beth's voice cracked. Tears shone in her eyes, and she wiped them away with balled fists. "How can you lie like that?"

Chris raised his eyebrows and shrugged, throwing his parents a bewildered look.

"What's going on here?" her mother asked.

"Nothing. Can I be excused?"

"You haven't eaten very much."

"I'm not hungry."

Rising from the table, Beth cleared her place and ran upstairs, flinging herself on the bed. Tears streamed and she buried her head in her pillow. "No one ever listens to me. They all think I'm a baby," she said in a muffled voice. Raising her head for air, she gave the pillow a punch and then cried until she was played out.

She grabbed a tissue from the nightstand and blew her nose. *What's wrong with Chris? Why is he acting like that?* Usually she and Chris got along all right, although he had changed recently. Now that he was thirteen, he paid more attention to how he looked and worried about what people thought of him. But that didn't explain what he did at dinner.

She went over recent events, starting with the move. Friends had been left behind. She started a new school, had a living nightmare, and shared an incredible dream with her brother. And then there was the light, the most amazing and disturbing experience of all. She wanted to share that experience.

"One thing's for sure," she muttered. "I won't tell Chris anything anymore. I don't need him." Luckily, Chris had to clean the yard whether he wanted to or not, and that gave her a degree of satisfaction. On Saturday, she would pay a visit to Mrs. Peasgood and ask her how to start gardening.

Chapter Fourteen

Portrait of a Dream

Emma Peasgood put the finishing touches on a lively watercolor of primroses. Sunlight flooded the studio, and the air from the open window, warmer than usual, carried a hint of spring.

Hearing a knock on the door, she rose to answer it, paintbrush in hand. "Beth, it's nice to see you. Please come in."

Beth noticed the paintbrush. "Are you painting right now? Is this a bad time?"

"Your timing is perfect. I was just thinking of making some tea. I'll clean my brushes first. Why don't you come and see my studio?"

Beth followed Mrs. Peasgood into a large room awash with light from many windows. Sketches and paintings filled all available space and were stacked on tables and floor. Framed paintings of flowers, forests, and animals added color to the white walls.

While Mrs. Peasgood cleaned her brushes, Beth moved along the wall of paintings. One painting in particular stood out, and she stopped dead in astonishment. The glowing birches and surrounding flowers left no doubt that this was the dream garden. Her heart hammered with excitement, and she stepped closer for a better look.

"It's how the garden looked at its best," Mrs. Peasgood said, stepping beside her. "Is something wrong?" she asked, noticing the stunned expression on Beth's face.

"No. It's just . . . " Beth hadn't intended to mention the dream. *But why not, why shouldn't I tell someone?*

"I had a dream about the garden exactly like your painting."

"Did you?"

"Actually, Chris and I both dreamed about it."

"I can see there's a story here," Mrs. Peasgood said. "We'll go in the kitchen for that tea, and you can tell me all about it."

With hands wrapped around a steaming mug, Beth told Mrs. Peasgood how she and Chris met in the garden, discovering that they were sharing a dream. "Everything seemed so real. I could even smell the flowers and feel the grass." Beth leaned in, looking Mrs. Peasgood in the eye. "The strangest thing is that we've never seen the garden, and your painting is exactly what we saw."

Mrs. Peasgood sat quietly for a moment before replying, and Beth felt uncertain. Her story sounded far-fetched, and Mrs. Peasgood might think she made it up.

"What an extraordinary experience."

Beth let out a long breath. "I wasn't sure you'd believe me."

"Why not? It seems that you, Chris, and I have all experienced something remarkable from the garden."

"Chris doesn't want to admit it, and you're the only one I can talk to. I tried to tell my parents, but Chris made me feel stupid."

"You can't change how Chris feels, and there's no point in worrying about it. But I'm curious about what you think. What do you want to do, if anything, about the dream and the light?"

"I want to be a gardener. I want the garden to be beautiful again."

"That's wonderful," Mrs. Peasgood said, with a bright smile. "Restoring the garden has some good news and some bad news. Which would you like to hear first?"

Beth returned her smile. "Let's start with the good news."

"Even though the overall condition of the garden is bad, there are a great many varieties of perennials that still bloom around the rubbish."

"What are perennials?"

"These are flowers that don't need to be planted every year. Some, like tulips, daffodils, and crocuses, come from bulbs. Others, like irises, come from rhizomes. The garden also has lilac bushes, which are quite hardy, and rose bushes, which are in rough shape."

"Now for the bad news."

"Gardening is hard work, and to be successful, you need

dedication."

"I really want to do this, but it's going to be hard without Chris's help."

"Just plug away, and don't set your sights too high," Mrs. Peasgood suggested. "Even a little gardening can yield beautiful results."

"How do I get started?"

"One thing you might consider is making a diagram of the area that you want to work on."

"By the birches, like in the painting."

"All right, I'll get the painting and we'll take a look."

She returned with the painting, a large sheet of paper, and some colored pencils. After propping the painting on a chair, she spread the paper on the table. "The roses are here and here," she said, drawing two circles with the red pencil. "We'll label them 'roses' and use the colored pencil that matches the flower color."

"And over here are the lilacs," Beth said, writing "lilac" in the purple circle she had drawn.

The finished diagram seemed accurate and gave a good reference from which to work.

"The yard still needs cleaning and raking," Beth said, "and Chris will have to help with that. It's his job."

"Next Saturday is spring break, and it also happens to be the first day of spring. I can't promise anything, but it's possible that you might have some helpers, at least for one day. My grandchildren are coming for a visit and might be persuaded to lend a hand."

"We could have a garden party," Beth suggested. "It sounds better than a work party. And we could have sandwiches and cake."

"If you'd like to arrange that," Mrs. Peasgood said, "I would be happy to supply the cake for the party."

"It's funny, but I've never been this excited about work before," Beth said.

Mrs. Peasgood nodded. "It's how you decide gardening will be. Some think of it as work, some choose to think of it as play."

Chapter Fifteen

Work It Out

Forget it. I don't want to work all day on Saturday, and I don't feel like meeting Mrs. Peasgood's grandchildren." Chris folded his arms and glared at Beth.

"Chris, you have a job to do," his father said, "and the sooner you tackle it, the sooner you'll have time for other things."

"I don't want to be a gardener."

"No one said you had to," Beth shot back.

They sat around the breakfast table, each with a hasty meal of toast or cereal.

"Gardening is Beth's project," their mother said, "and I think it's a terrific idea. We should be supportive."

Beth couldn't help feeling smug and offered Chris a bright smile.

"Whatever is going on between you two, I suggest you work it out," their father snapped. "It's too early in the morning to put up with your troubles."

Chris and Beth looked sullen.

"Are you riding with us today or taking the bus?" Their mother asked, filling a thermos of coffee and gathering her things.

"Ride."

"Bus."

"Why don't you both take the bus. That will give you time, before it gets here, to iron things out."

They mumbled goodbyes to their parents and waited until they heard the car pull out of the driveway.

"Why did you have to blab about the dream?" Chris asked. He shoved a sandwich into a paper bag and then fired in some cookies.

"What's the big deal? It happened."

"Yes, it happened, but that's as far as I want to go."

"Why?"

"What do you think people will say if you start spouting off about lights and magic?"

"I knew it. You're afraid of what people will think."

"Now you've got it. I'm older than you. I have new friends to hang out with, and we won't be talking about magic. That stuff's for babies." Chris picked up his lunch. "Are you coming?" He threw on his jacket and went outside.

"I'm not a baby," she called out to the closing door. And then more quietly, "If you can't believe what's right in front of your face, it's too bad for you."

Chapter Sixteen

The Peasgood Kids

Bird chatter through the open window roused Beth from sleep. *I should have closed that,* she thought. Chilled air streamed in and she gathered the blankets closer, sinking down into the warmth. From her cozy nest, she watched the cloudless sky. *It's a perfect day for the garden party.*

Quickly dressing, she went downstairs, finding to her surprise that everyone was seated at the table eating breakfast.

"Hi, sleepyhead, pull up a chair." Her mother slid a chair out from the table with her foot.

"I thought you were all still sleeping."

"Not today, there's too much to do." Her mother said. "If you want some pancakes, you'd better hurry. Chris is eyeing what's left."

"A person needs a few perks for working on a Saturday," he said, stabbing one from the stack. "Pancakes count for one perk. I guess lunch counts for another."

"And the satisfaction of a clean yard," his father said.

"Sure, that too." Chris displayed little enthusiasm, but he knew there would be no getting out of yard work today. "So, what's the plan?" he asked.

"You and Beth are in the yard," his father said, "raking up the dead grass and removing the rest of the junk. We've arranged for the old truck to be towed this afternoon, and the bags of trash will be hauled to the dump."

"Has anyone heard from Mrs. Peasgood?" Beth asked.

"Her grandchildren have agreed to help and will be here within the hour," her father said.

"And that's it for me, right? No more yard work after today," Chris said.

"If you finish today, yes," his father said. "You do realize that there will always be chores to do."

"I know. I just don't feel like planting flowers." He gave Beth a pointed look.

"I can handle that part on my own," she said.

"Since this is the first party at our new house, your Dad and I will make a special lunch."

"That sounds great," Beth said. "I'm ready to start."

"Okay, let's go," Chris said. "I'm going to finish collecting up the trash, and you can rake." Without waiting to see if this suited Beth, he rose from his seat and slipped out the door.

She didn't mind raking, but felt peeved that Chris was taking charge. This was her garden party, after all. She swallowed her irritation and followed Chris out into the yard.

The raking fell into a steady rhythm, and the dead grass lifted easily, revealing a thin carpet of young sprouts. As she completed an area, she paused to admire the finished results.

Chris walked by hauling some junk up to the garage. "I really don't want to be doing this," he grumbled.

She was about to fire back a suitable remark when she spotted three children walking toward them, a girl and two boys. The girl appeared to be as tall as Chris, and Beth guessed her age at twelve or thirteen. The small boy could be six or seven, she decided, and the other boy looked closer to her own age.

"Hi, I'm Lindsey, and these are my brothers, Andrew and Alex."

Beth started to introduce herself, but Chris stepped in with a huge smile.

"Hi, I'm Chris, and this is my sister Beth."

"Grams said that you were having a garden party," Lindsey said, "but you really need help working in the yard."

"That's true, we do need help," Chris said, "but it's a party too. We'll have a good lunch, a picnic really, and your grandmother is bringing the cake."

"Okay," Lindsey said, "Besides, I like gardening."

"Me too," Chris said.

Beth geared up to dispute that statement, but changed her mind. *If it takes a pretty girl with long copper colored hair to keep Chris working, I'll keep quiet.*

She looked at Andrew. His wavy hair curled around his ears in a burnished copper hue. Freckles dusted his nose. When he noticed her scrutiny, his face lit in a wide smile. Alex was simply a smaller version.

"Sure, we'll help," Andrew said. "What do you want us to do?"

Everyone worked at a variety of jobs throughout the morning. Alex took an instant liking to Beth and became her constant companion.

"How old are you?" he asked.

"Eleven."

"I'm almost seven," he volunteered. Then he launched into topics of super heroes, comics, and cartoons.

The morning passed quickly, and the yard transformed before their eyes.

Chapter Seventeen

Ritual of the Equinox

Sunshine ushered in the first day of spring, and the warming soil cast a vigorous earthy scent. Birds, busy with the affairs of breakfast, tugged earthworms from the loam.

Fairies assembled throughout the garden. They awaited the first strains of music, signaling the Ritual of the Equinox. Clear notes sounded, and the dancers stepped forward.

The Birtknocks of Turtle Valley were the masters of dance. Beginning with a simple step, their tapping feet brought awareness to sleeping seeds and bulbs, buried in the earth. More intricate rhythms produced steady bursts of joy, coaxing the seedlings to open. Music compelled tiny sprouts to push through the soil.

As often as Thornby had experienced this, he would never grow used to the wonder of the ceremony. He loved the artistry of the dancers and musicians, and how the plants responded to their care.

He produced a small fiddle and drew his bow across the strings. Smiling at the resonant tone, he played a melody gentle as spring rain. Tender shoots drank in the nourishing sound, and hardly noticeable at first, they began to grow, their transparency giving way to rich golden green.

The tune completed, Thornby stepped back to appreciate the new plants dotting the soil, among them crocuses, hyacinth, and daffodils. Later in the day, after the plants had rested, the pipers and singers would assist in the shaping of the buds. That completed the Equinox Ritual, to be followed with feasting, music, and dance at the great hall.

Artemus joined Thornby as he put away his fiddle.

"Wonderful morning," Artemus greeted Thornby with a smile. He looked far more energetic than their last meeting. "When those dancers wake the seeds, I feel like I'll crack apart, just from the joy of it." He smiled and pointed over Thornby's shoulder. "Those children are out there working in the garden, and they've been joined by others. I have to admit that you were right. Even with the little they've done so far, I feel much more awake, not so muddled."

"Good thing," Thornby said, "because we're all looking forward to tomorrow when the colors are unveiled."

Artemus was a poet, one of the best. Although with the decline of the garden, he had suffered a "dry spell," he felt up to the task that lay ahead. In fact, he looked forward to it.

Chapter Eighteen

The Garden Party

Come and get it."

"Lunch, let's go." Beth dropped her rake and joined the others in a race for the house.

The porch, brightly transformed, had the look of a gypsy caravan. Tables were draped with festive cloths, laden with food. Mrs. Peasgood had already arrived with the promised cake, which sat invitingly in a prominent spot.

"A job well done," Mrs. Peasgood said, by way of greeting.

"Hi Grams," Alex shouted, as the children charged up the steps. "Wow, look at all the food."

Chris introduced Lindsey, Andrew, and Alex to his parents, who were sitting with Mrs. Peasgood.

"You've all done a remarkable job," Chris's father said. "It's hard to believe I'm looking at the same yard. Volunteering to help was very thoughtful," he said to Mrs. Peasgood's grandchildren. "Now, if you'd care to wash up, we'll begin the party."

Beth reached for a bowl, stacked beside a steaming pot of soup, and ladled in the broth, thick with vegetables.

"Mmm, grilled cheese sandwiches," Lindsey said, "My favorite."

"We like them too," Beth said. "Mom always lays out different things to add on," she pointed to a variety of bowls, "like tomatoes, avocado, and jalapeno jelly. The jelly is too hot for me, but Chris likes it."

When the children had filled their plates, they retreated to the yard where, true to picnic fashion, blankets had been placed on the ground. Cold seeped through them, but no one cared. A picnic in March was very appealing. The grown-ups elected to stay on the porch where there were comfortable chairs.

"It's great that you've moved in," Andrew said, sitting cross-legged on the blanket. "We don't know too many people around here."

"How often do you visit your grandmother?" Chris asked.

"Usually for spring break and for six weeks in the summer. When we come, we'll bring our bikes and show you some great trails for riding."

"Swimming too," Lindsey said, "and we'll also take you to the falls."

"I'm going for cake," Alex announced, gathering up his dishes.

"Me too." Beth said, and followed him to the table.

Mrs. Peasgood cut the cake into generous portions, giving each of them a piece.

"This looks good," Beth said.

"It's from an old family recipe," Mrs. Peasgood said. "My mother used to make it, and it was always my favorite, banana pecan with fudge frosting."

Beth noticed with surprise that Alex took two more helpings, even though he hadn't touched the first piece. He reached for some napkins, wrapped the cakes, and turning away, walked back to where they had been working. Curious, she followed.

He unwrapped the cakes and placed them on the stone steps.

"What are you doing?" she asked.

"I'm leaving cakes for the fairies," he said.

Beth started, "Fairies, have you seen fairies?"

"No, but Grams said it's always good to leave a gift."

Late in the afternoon, Beth and Chris saw a tow truck wheel into the yard. A large man in a red-checked jacket stepped out and talked to their father, who pointed. The man returned to his truck and rumbled down the hill.

"He's going to run over the stone steps." Beth shouted. "Quick, we have to stop him."

"Why bother? The steps are falling apart anyway," Chris said.

Beth sped down the hill as fast as she could run, but the truck was too far ahead. It belched a plume of exhaust, heading straight for the embankment.

She stopped, and helplessly looked on.

The tow truck crushed some new plants, sprouting alongside, but the steps, themselves were left intact, with only inches to spare.

With a groan, the old truck lurched from its nest of bushes. It thumped along on flat tires, disappearing over the hill in a cloud of blue.

Maeve stretched out upon her bed of moss. Like all fairies, she had taken part in the Ritual of the Equinox. *It went well,* she thought with satisfaction, *especially the area I worked on.* Her clear voice had shaped well-formed buds, giving them the start they needed, to produce the best colors the following morning.

After all the activity of the day, the quiet of her room lured her to sleep. "Just a short nap," she murmured, closing her eyes. The feast was still a few hours away.

With a life of its own, the bed lurched, throwing her to the floor. Only it wasn't just the bed, the whole house pitched. Fumes and loud rumbling filled the room.

"My house," she shrieked. "They're stealing my house." She attempted to stand, only to be knocked down by a second jolt. Lifting her head, she looked around the room, thinking of her possessions. *There's no time for that,* she thought. *I've got to get out now.*

The truck shuddered violently and pulled forward. Sick at heart, she quickly crawled toward the door, but a glint from her reflecting glass brought her up short. "I won't leave this behind," she cried, and grasped it, before leaping to safety.

Chapter Nineteen

The Unveiling

The festively decorated hall did not reflect the feelings of shock and dismay. Some fairies stood off by themselves, others gathered in small groups, speaking quietly. The day had gone well only to end in disaster. Worry over Maeve's whereabouts was on everyone's mind.

Chief Councilor Vali stood before the milling fairies unsure of how to proceed. Finally, calling for their attention, he began.

"Friends, we have had a most successful day. The Ritual of the Equinox surpassed our greatest expectations, only to be marred by that unfortunate incident. Despite this, I feel we must continue the momentum generated today. As to the humans, Thornby assures me that he will take care of the problem. Thornby?" He motioned for Thornby to approach.

"Much has been accomplished by the human children in a very short time," Thornby said. "Keep in mind that our contact with them has been limited. They are not aware of our needs and expectations. Indeed, it is likely that they are not aware of us at all."

"What can be done about that?" shouted one of the pipers from the back of the hall.

"I will meet them if I can. It's worth a try."

"What about Maeve?" someone asked in a quiet voice. "How can you fix that? And where is she?"

"Maeve tends to be a bit solitary, and with the loss she has suffered, I suspect she'll need to be alone for a while," Thornby said. "One thing we could do is build a new house for her, perhaps a bower."

"I don't think Maeve would be happy in a bower," the piper called out.

"It's very different from the truck, and that can't be helped,"

Thornby said, "but, furnishing it with unique and beautiful things would help to ease her loss. Any who are interested in building Maeve's house, please see me later."

He has developed into quite a leader of late, Vali thought, stepping beside Thornby. "Thank you, Thornby," he said. "We will leave these problems in your capable hands. Food, music, and dance await. Let's celebrate our accomplishments today and prepare ourselves for the Unveiling of the Colors in the morning. So please, enjoy the evening."

Food piled high on the tables beckoned. Among the fare was an exotic cake covered in a dark, sweet substance. "Brought by the children," Thornby was informed. *Does this mean that they are aware of us?* he wondered.

The offering of cake did much to ease the tension concerning the humans, and the fairies were happy to leave the problem to Thornby.

The poets moved softly. Each selected a group of plants and settled among the newly formed buds. In quiet anticipation, the fairies stood watching, as the poets prepared for the Unveiling of the Colors.

Artemus sat with eyes closed, gathering his words in silence. With simplicity, he revealed all aspects of garden life—the sun, rain, and soil—and the loving care of the fairies. Each word fell upon the plants, gently washing over the buds, moving along the stems, and settling around the tender roots.

"You are delicate expressions of Nature. Together you are the garden. As individuals, each supports the other, contributing their best. By deeply drawing from yourselves, exquisite color and scent will manifest, and the joy of your being will lift the spirits of all who behold your gifts."

The skill of the poets was such that by the timbre of their voices and the power of their words, they set in motion a resonating sound that thrummed in the plants, reaching inside where their deepest beauty lay. In that way, the plants pushed out the richest of their chosen color.

Slowly, the buds opened, unfolding petals of radiant yellow, vibrant blues and violets, delicate pink, and the softest white.

The fairies welcomed the flowers, surrounding them with love.

"Well done," Juniper said, joining Artemus. "The colors are magnificent."

"Thank you," he said.

They stood quietly for a while, drinking in the freshness of the day and the vitality of the flowers.

Chapter Twenty

Payback

Maeve raged. She ran steadily, fueled by her anger. Only in the dimness of approaching night did she waver. The fields and rolling hills were gone, and she found, to her surprise, that she had entered a dense forest. Massive cedars closed in and fallen trees lay rotting across her path, draped in beards of phosphorescent moss.

Rage is truly blind, she thought. *Where am I?* A wave of exhaustion swept over her, and spotting a large rock, she sat, leaning against its cold surface. *Now what?* No answer presented itself. Sitting in silence as the last light faded, she felt empty and alone. As if it could provide companionship, she hugged her reflecting glass, and burrowing down into dry grass, she fell asleep.

Sunlight surfaced above the rock and Maeve woke with a start. Judging by the sun's height, she had slept long. Yesterday's events jolted her memory and she groaned. *This is Thornby's and Juniper's fault, and those children's. Involving them was a disaster. We don't need a midsummer celebration. Everything was fine the way it was.*

She stood abruptly and paced, bombarded with the pain of her loss. *The preparation for midsummer is about to be ruined,* she decided. *The question is how?* She stopped pacing. An idea ignited, bringing a smile to her lips. *I'll approach the imps. They thrive on chaos. In fact, seeking their help would be doing them a favor.* The seeds of revenge found fertile soil in her heart.

Maeve determined her general location by the sun's position. *The imp kingdom lies to the west, perhaps a few days' journey from here,* she thought. The more she considered the imps, the more convinced she was that they would help. However, before starting out, she had to look to her immediate needs. Plucking some dry grass, she deftly wove a carry bag. It was large enough to accommodate her reflecting glass, as well as any seeds or roots she might find along the way.

The morning was nearly over by the time she set out. Slinging the carry bag over her shoulder, she broke into a trot, eager to put some distance behind her. She maintained a steady pace, slowing only when an obstacle presented itself. Dense foliage often forced her to change directions, and she clenched her teeth with frustration. *If I were a frebble fairy I'd have wings,* she thought. *Bad trade-off, though, they're such empty-heads.*

Late in the afternoon, Maeve discovered a deer trail, which ran in the desired direction. Thereafter, her progress improved. The forest fell behind and the trail descended sharply. It led through thick stands of aspen, still bare from the long winter. Shoots of avalanche lilies poked through the grass, and she knelt to dig a few bulbs.

The sound of running water heightened her growing thirst. Leaving the trail, she soon spotted a stream cascading, clear and icy, from the heights. *This is a good place to stop for the night,* she thought.

Maeve reached into her bag and pulled out the avalanche lilies. Taking a long drink from the stream, she then washed the dirt from the bulbs. A rock overhang provided good shelter, and she set about making a bed of grass in the shadowed trough below. Satisfied, she bit into a lily bulb and gave more thought to her plan.

Imps preferred isolation, and she had to consider the best way to approach them. Occasionally, they could be spotted away from their realm, usually in a raiding party. These forays involved stealing, or causing some other mischief.

She wasn't even sure of the location of their kingdom, except that it lay to the west. If she wandered in that direction, the imps would very likely find her. It was well known that the imps guarded their realm closely.

I have to make my request sound attractive, she thought. Certainly the chance to disrupt the celebration would be irresistible, but accepting her as an outsider might be difficult. *I can be charming,* she thought, glossing over the queasiness of doubt in her stomach. *They'll take me in, no doubt about it.* Maeve settled in for the night.

After a quick wash and another bite of lily bulb, she returned to the trail, pleased with the early start. It wasn't long before the slope leveled off. The trail, pocked with deer tracks, led to a pond, leaving her westerly direction cut off.

She had to choose between north and south. From her position, it was difficult to see the shortest way around. The north side appeared more open, but to the south, the trail looked well used. She headed south. Soon the ground became marshy and the going slowed. As the day wore on, she had little to show for her efforts.

"Stop right there," said a voice.

Maeve froze.

"No one travels here without permission from the king." An imp stepped from a thicket of brush.

Her face blanched at the imposing figure, standing at twice her height. "I'm here to ask . . ."

"There will be no talking," he barked, "until you have leave from the king." His hand clamped on Maeve's arm, and he yanked her forward.

Chapter Twenty-one

Double-Edged Hospitality

Maeve studied her captor with growing alarm. He had a powerful presence. A thatch of bright red hair stood stiffly from his crown, coarsely falling like a horsetail down his back. His clothes, curiously iridescent, sparkled with light when he moved. Maeve walked beside him in silence.

By the time they reached the imp settlement, night had fallen. She heard the rushing sound of a stream somewhere in the darkness. Guessing that it led back to the pond, she decided it would be a good escape route if needed.

They clamored over rocks, finally entering an opening at the base of a granite wall. Light baskets were set at intervals, illuminating the way with a greenish cast. The tunnel in which they traveled took many turns. Maeve lost count of the secondary tunnels and chambers, realizing that she would not be able to find her way out. Several imps passed by. None spoke, but their smiles caused her to shiver.

Eventually the tunnel opened into a brilliantly lit hall. Maeve blinked at the intensity. With wonder, she saw that the entire ceiling had been tiled with mica, reflecting the glow from the light baskets. The imps, like the fairies, collected light from fireflies, and had certainly found a clever way to use it.

Crowds of imps filled the hall. They seemed to glow themselves as light bounced off their iridescent clothing, but none so radiant as the king and queen.

Maeve stood straight with her chin up. There was no choice but to go through with this ordeal, and she would do so with dignity.

The imp led her to the foot of the dais. The king, engaged in conversation, took a moment to notice her. However, the queen's hard stare settled upon Maeve and then on her carry bag. Instinctively, she tightened her grip on her reflecting glass. At this, the queen raised an eyebrow and smiled coldly.

"Bow to the king and queen," the imp said. With his hand on her back, he forced her over, bowing himself as well. The king turned his head and nodded, acknowledging his due respect.

"Your majesty, I found this one skulking about by the pond."

Seething with indignation, Maeve held herself in check. She knew that everything hinged on making a good impression, and this fool of an imp was making her look bad.

"Well done, Bracken," the king said, "You are dismissed."

The imp took three steps backward, bowed, and turning smartly, strode from the hall.

"And who might you be?" the king asked, turning his attention to Maeve.

She drew herself up and replied in a clear voice, "I am Maeve, and I have come to ask . . ."

"I will ask the questions here," the king snapped. "It is rare to see a lone fairy. How is it that you have come to my hall?"

"My home was destroyed. Humans and fairies were involved, and now I have nowhere to go."

"It is not an uncommon practice among the humans to destroy."

"The fairies had a hand . . ."

He silenced her with a look. "This is an unlikely place for you to travel," he said. "Cousins though we are, there are great differences between us. If you are looking to us for help, you will not find it. Your troubles are of no interest to us."

The assembled imps were eager to learn the fate of the lone fairy. Hoping for some amusement, they pressed in from all sides.

Maeve's mouth went dry. She fought the urge to bolt, useless as that would be, and said, "I seek revenge."

"Revenge is it?" the king smiled, "How unfairy-like."

The queen leaned forward. "I want to see what she carries in that bag."

This was too much for Maeve. She clutched the reflecting glass to her chest. "No," she said, more forcefully than she'd intended.

An audible intake of breath hissed through the crowd. Shocked and angry at her impertinence, they surged forward.

"I invoke the rights of hospitality!" she demanded, surprised by her own strength.

The king held up his hand. "You have it," he nodded, grudgingly. "We are bound by those laws. You may keep your possessions."

"Thank you," Maeve said with relief.

The king settled into his chair. His arm fell to the side, absently stroking a salamander, which lay curled on the floor. "We will talk further tomorrow," he said. "Now we eat."

Instantly, trestle tables were produced, and Maeve was ushered to a bench. She had a clear view of the king and queen, and while the food was carried to the tables, she used the time to study her hosts. They sat deep in conversation, the queen clearly upset. *I had better be cautious,* she thought.

The queen wore a dress of the iridescent material that many of the imps preferred. It shimmered at every turn, and the fit of the dress enhanced her great height, matching that of the king. With shock, Maeve realized that the iridescent clothing was made of snakeskin. At once the differences in their cultures became apparent.

She watched the food being placed on the table with a rush of apprehension. The imp cuisine did not appear to be fruits and vegetables. (All fairies are vegetarian.) Sure enough, the first of the steaming platters was unidentifiable.

The imp to her right offered her a ladle full of a dark, marshy-smelling substance. "Poached tadpole, smothered in a rich juniper berry sauce," he said, proudly, pouring it into her bowl. "Of course it's seasonal, one of the great pleasures of spring."

The law of hospitality is double edged, Maeve thought. *I must accept everything graciously. One must never insult the host.* She smiled her thanks, struggling for a way to avoid her duty. The next platter, to her relief, contained a crusty bread, made from cattail pollen.

"You must try some steamed water plants," said the same imp,

"Indigenous only to our area."

Clearly, the imp took the rules of hospitality seriously. His duty was to uphold the reputation of the king as a good host. Although the imp's manners were impeccable, his demeanor was formal and distant.

She made a good show of eating the bread, finding it surprisingly flavorful. Then she poked at the water plants taking a little nibble. The stringy greens imparted an oily, muddy flavor. *These are probably nutritious,* she thought, choking down a mouthful.

She could wait no longer. Black shiny tadpoles clumped in her bowl. Steeling herself, she lifted the spoon to her lips. The reeking smell nearly overwhelmed her.

"What . . .?" she cried out, dropping her spoon to the floor. Something cool brushed against her, and she drew her legs up onto the bench. A hasty look under the table showed three salamanders snapping at one another, competing for table scraps. Smiling to herself, Maeve joined the imps, dropping tadpole, bit by bit, until it was gone.

"What a delicious meal," she said, glad that it was over.

Serving imps removed the platters, replacing them with clay bowls of mead. With just one sip, the sweet honey liquor surged warmth through her body. Another bowl was set before her.

"Dessert," the imp smiled.

How bad can it be? she thought.

"Mosquito larvae pudding," the imp informed, "another spring delicacy."

No way out this time, she thought. Taking a gulp of mead, she gamely ate the pudding.

All imp eyes turned in her direction, following the motion of each spoonful. After she had emptied her bowl, the hall erupted in laughter, many imps nodding with approval. It dawned on her that the imps were well aware of her vegetarian diet, having fun at her expense.

Musicians appeared with an array of exotic instruments, arranging themselves on a woven mat. They played a lively piece, completely foreign to Maeve. Skilled fingers plucked stringed instruments of wood, brightly decorated and carved. Small cymbals and drums accompanied the music, which she found stirring, almost haunting.

The music flowed seamlessly, and it was difficult to tell when one song ended and another began. After the last note had faded, the imps thundered their approval.

"Well done," the king said, rising from his chair. He looked at Maeve. "Show our guest to her quarters." He offered his hand to the queen, and together they left the hall.

Two imps appeared on either side of Maeve and escorted her to her chamber.

"Thank you," she said, and stepped behind a curtain of woven marsh grass.

The room reflected a soft glow, illuminated by a single light basket. Although sparsely furnished, it offered surprising comfort. Intricately patterned carpets adorned the walls and floor. These, she discovered, were also woven with marsh grass, but dyed with many colors.

An alcove for washing and dressing contained a red clay water jug and bowl, and all the necessities for starting the day. In the sitting area stood a stone table and two stone benches, covered with colorful pillows. The bed was mounted high on the wall, its frame supported by three pieces of wood. These were buried deep into the rock wall and cemented with spruce pitch.

Deeply tired, Maeve climbed the ladder to the cradle-like bed and to her delight found it filled with cattail fluff. She nestled into grateful comfort. Closing her eyes, she placed a hand on the reflecting glass, tucked safely beside her.

Chapter Twenty-two

A Second Chance

She wouldn't be a gardener after all. Beth couldn't say why, but the idea of gardening had lost its charm. Guilt wormed its way in, which didn't make sense. Who was she hurting? Her energy sank to a listless, "don't want to do anything," feeling. Not even compliments on the great job could tweak her interest. She felt nothing. No focus, no ideas, no drive—just flat.

The week passed at a sluggish pace. When she thought about how the day went or what they had covered in class, she only remembered the slow stretches of time. A few opportunities came up to hang out with some of her classmates, but she bowed out. Didn't feel like it.

Saturday unfolded with nothing to do. Not that she wanted to do anything. Chris had a friend he'd met at school visiting, "Bobby-something". They sat on the sofa playing video games. Her parents were in the kitchen painting cupboards. *I'd better get out of here or they'll find a job for me,* she thought.

Using the front door to avoid the kitchen, she circled around to the back and wandered down the hill. Deep tire marks scarred the embankment beside the stone steps, and newly sprouted plants lay flattened. The truck had left a trail of ruts going down, and then again, going back up. She pictured the truck trundling off in a haze of blue smoke. That was when everything had changed, she realized.

Absentmindedly, she kicked a few clods of dirt into the trough, tamping it down with her foot.

"It's a start," said a voice.

Beth whirled around but saw no one.

"The problem is that you have lost our support."

She gaped with astonishment when a tiny figure emerged from

under a bush. Its form wavered, blinking in and out.

Not grasping what her eyes took in, she stammered, "I . . . What . . . ?"

"I'm a fairy. I'm not used to appearing before humans. Out of practice, you understand. It's difficult to remain visible." As if to prove his point, his little form flickered. Beth started to speak, but he stopped her with a gesture and closed his eyes in concentration. After a moment, some inner adjustment or fine-tuning stabilized his appearance.

She could see him clearly. His height looked to be five or six inches at most. Brown wavy hair fell to his shoulders, and his delicate facial features were drawn in a frown. "A fairy," she whispered in awe.

"This is a difficult time," he said, getting right to the point. "The future could go either way."

"What do you mean?"

"We have been working with you children in a spirit of cooperation, and a very productive day ended in disaster."

"The old truck," Beth said, her voice faint.

"Exactly." He crossed his arms with emphasis.

"I don't understand. Wouldn't the yard look better without the rusty old truck?"

"Yes it would," he said, "but if you are going to make changes, you have to tell us. We need time to make preparations of our own. And where's the cooperation if you make all of the decisions?"

"I'm very sorry. I had no idea."

"Just remember to inform us of your intentions. If you do, we shall support you once again."

"How do I do that?"

"Stand where you are now and speak. And one more thing, could you leave a bit of red cloth and a reflecting glass on the stone steps?"

"Reflecting glass, do you mean a mirror?"

"Mirr-or." He rolled the word around his mouth. "Yes, that's right, a mirror."

A thought popped into her head, and she stifled a giggle. She wondered if he had pointy ears and wished she could push his hair back to take a peek.

Beth had many questions, but could tell that he was ready to leave. "Will I see you again?" she asked, stalling his departure.

"It's possible."

"I'm Beth."

"You honor me with your true name, but it isn't wise to give it out carelessly. You may call me by my everyday name, Thornby."

"Why shouldn't I say my name?"

"I don't understand this human habit. Revealing your true name can be dangerous. It can give power over you to those who hear it." He looked worried. "Have you seen or heard anything unusual since moving in?"

"Everything has been unusual."

Thornby smiled. "I suppose so. Just be cautious," he said, and vanished.

"He exploded," Rill shouted with glee. He and Strega stood behind the boys riveted to the action on the television. They had realized quickly that the boys were playing a game, but they didn't care. All the destruction was highly entertaining.

Their fingers twitched, longing to take over the controls. "Yes!" they cheered as the characters exploded. Hero or enemy, it didn't matter.

"If this is the nature of their games, our assignment will be quick," Strega said. "I get nothing from the game, but the boys are pumping out some good aggression." A thrill of power coursed through the wiggins. "I like this world."

Chapter Twenty-three

Acting Out

The powerful contrast from emptiness to fullness blasted through her, and she felt blessed. *It's a gift,* she thought. *A gift.* Those words brought back another vision, clouding the moment. *Yes, but that was a dream,* she told herself.

The first impulse insisted she burst through the door shouting "fairies in the garden." However, experience suggested caution.

A stench filled her nostrils as she stepped through the door. She saw two shadowy figures hovering over Chris and Bobby. Beth stood for a moment in shock, and the joy she had felt only a moment ago gave way to fury. She snapped.

"Get out," she screamed.

They turned to face her, distorted features pulled back in a lipless grin.

At the same time Chris and Bobby jumped off the sofa.

"What's the matter with you?" Chris shouted.

"I said get out," Beth ignored Chris and pointed to the door.

The wiggins grew taller, towering over the boys, and Beth backed up. A thought bolted through her brain. The existence of fairies meant this nightmare was also true.

Her parents ran from the kitchen.

"What's happening here?" her mother cried.

"Don't you see them?" Beth desperately needed them to see.

"Bobby, I think you'd better go home now." Her mother's chin lifted toward the door.

Bobby grabbed his jacket and gave Beth a wide berth. "Freak," he muttered under his breath, and left.

"Thanks a lot, Beth." Chris shouldered past her and slammed the door, following Bobby.

The shapes thickened, and the shadows pulled back revealing

their full form. They stood tall, with long limbs. Yellow eyes regarded Beth from sunken faces. Long, thin noses curved toward their gaping mouths, showing sharp, yellowed teeth. Leather garments hung in shreds from their bodies. Their smell spoke of decay.

Beth's eyes fell on claws that could rip her family apart, but why were they just standing there? Her fists clenched in a surge of anger, and a cry rasped from deep within her throat "Leave us alone and don't come back."

"Beth, stop it right now." Her father took her by the arm and marched her straight to her room.

"You were rude to Chris and Bobby, and talking to someone who isn't there is a child's game. Are you still a baby? Stay in your room and think about what you've done. And I expect an apology to Chris."

Later when she walked to the bathroom, she heard her parents talking downstairs. She paused by the railing and looked down. They sat together discussing what had happened. The two creatures were still there. One sat at the end of the couch beside her mother, looking comfortable, his feet propped on the coffee table. The other sprawled in an easy chair. She pulled away from the railing before they spotted her and listened.

"She's seeing things, Steven. This is serious. Is she mentally ill? Is she schizophrenic?"

"Come on, Annie, she's just acting out. She's angry that we moved here, and this is a creative way to throw us off. Let's give it time and she'll get tired of her little game."

"It's not fair, Steven. The store is opening in a week. Our lives are stressful enough without this."

Beth saw the creatures look at each other with surprise and then they disappeared.

"Steven? Annie? I thought their names were 'Steve' and 'Anne.' This is no good, no good at all. If the names aren't right, we can't use them." Rill said.

"Maybe we won't have to," Strega said. "Beth and Chris can supply all we need."

After breakfast on Sunday morning, Beth considered Thornby's request. She remembered the makeup compact her grandmother Margaret had used. Whenever they were going somewhere, her grandmother asked them to wait while she "put on her face." She had given the compact to Beth to play with when the makeup was gone. Beth thought the round, golden case with a mirror inside would be perfect. She wanted the red cloth to be special too and took scissors to a red velvet dress she'd outgrown. *A hand-me-down for fairies*, Beth thought, cutting a tidy square.

When no one was looking, she slipped out the kitchen door and walked down the hill to the stone steps. She placed the folded velvet on the bottom step with the opened compact on top and walked away.

Chapter Twenty-four

Payment

Maeve awoke with a start.

"You have been summoned," an imp called from the door.

"One moment." She lowered herself over the edge of the bed, padded to the door, and drew back the curtain.

"You have been summoned," he repeated. "Be in the hall within the hour." He turned smartly on his heel, heading back down the corridor with long, sweeping strides.

Water from the pitcher washed away the last traces of sleep. A clean dress had been left to replace her soiled clothes. *They must have brought it while I slept,* she thought, not liking the idea. The soft garment was not made of snakeskin, and she was pleasantly surprised with the comfortable fit. Properly attired, Maeve felt ready for her audience with the king.

"Ah, there you are," the king said. "I trust you were comfortable in your quarters?"

"Yes, your majesty, thank you." She bowed.

The queen did not speak, but regarded her with interest. Maeve cautioned herself to be on guard.

"Let us begin," the king said in a business-like manner. "What exactly do you want from us?"

"There is an upcoming celebration on the summer solstice. The fairies have enlisted the help of humans, and together they are working to ready the garden. As part of that effort, and without any thought to my well-being, my home was torn away like so much refuse." Maeve's throat tightened. "No one tried to stop it. I, myself, barely escaped, and everything I value is lost."

"How unfortunate," the king sympathized.

"Yes, unfortunate," the queen said.

72

Anger flared as Maeve explained her situation. Her voice became louder. "I want the fairies to feel the loss that I have suffered. I want them to realize . . ."

"Yes, yes," the queen cut her off, drumming her fingers with boredom. "What do you propose?"

The queen's indifference pulled the plug, and Maeve's anger drained away. She took a deep breath to steady her resolve. "I want to spoil the celebration. When the guests arrive, the fairies will be humiliated. We can make it look like the humans did it." Her eyes kindled with self-righteousness, and her voice again grew stronger. "They will learn that they can never count on humans. And I must teach them this for their own good."

A spark of interest lit the king's eyes, and he smiled. "That's where we come in. You want us to carry out your revenge."

The word "revenge" sounded harsh uttered by the imp king.

"Well, yes," she said, suddenly worried. Was she starting something that might get out of hand? "Don't misunderstand me. The fairies are family and friends. I don't want to hurt them or destroy the garden—just teach them a much needed lesson."

"Hurt the fairies? Destroy the garden? What do you take us for?" the king demanded. His face reddened. "We are not evil, cousin. We simply enjoy a bit of fun now and then." He reached for the queen's hand, calming noticeably. "Is that not so, my dear?"

"It is." Her gaze leveled on Maeve.

"No need to worry. You can leave everything to us." The king said. "I have an idea that may prove amusing. There is no need to thank us," the king held up his hand when Maeve moved to speak. "We will accept our payment now."

Maeve paled. She didn't think a fee would be involved.

"What treasure have you brought to finance this project?" the king asked.

"No doubt it is in your bag," the queen said, her eyes glinting with triumph.

And there you have it, Maeve thought, *after everything I have endured, the reflecting glass will also be lost.* "Yes, it is in my bag."

The queen snapped her fingers and sent an imp to retrieve Maeve's bag from her room. In no time the imp returned, handing the bag to Maeve.

Sitting forward, the queen eagerly watched as Maeve withdrew her precious glass. Its clear surface gathered light to itself, sending forth a dazzling radiance.

The queen drew in her breath. "Bring it to me." Examining the reflecting glass, the queen started in surprise. Her own face peered back, regal and beautiful. Of course, she had been aware of her beauty. A glimpse in the pond had confirmed it. But this! Clearly, she was far more beautiful than even she had thought. Arrested by her own image, the mirror commanded her attention.

"You have brought us a treasure indeed," The king said, well pleased. "We will work out the details of our enterprise. Until you return to your homeland, you will be our honored guest."

The queen never once looked up from the reflecting glass.

Chapter Twenty-five

The Grand Opening

Throngs of people filled the store. Beth stood under the "Brinson Bookstore Grand Opening" banner, manning the punch bowl and replenishing a sumptuous array of nibbles as the platters emptied. A familiar face emerged from the crowd.

"Can I offer you some punch, Mrs. Peasgood?"

"Thank you, Beth. Everything looks so good."

Beth ladled some punch into a cup and handed it to Mrs. Peasgood. "I'm glad you could come," she said.

"I wouldn't miss it. Our little town has been sorely in need of a bookstore. Those look good." Mrs. Peasgood set down her cup and reached for a cookie. "Did you make them?" she asked, breaking off a corner and popping it into her mouth.

"No, Chris made those. I made the brownies."

"Then I must have one of each."

A press of people gathered behind Mrs. Peasgood, lining up for punch. She quickly drained her cup, picked up a brownie, and winked at Beth. "I'm off to explore."

When the demand for punch slackened, Beth left her post to have a better look at the store. She had seen it a few times as the store was taking shape, but hadn't had a chance to see it finished. Books lined the walls, and freestanding shelves created corridors. A chair sat at the end of each row.

Potted palm trees flanked the entrance to the children's area. The faint sound of African drums lent an air of expectancy as Beth entered the room. Her parents had given special thought to the children's section, deciding on an African theme. Mosquito netting draped from the ceiling. A pair of giraffes thundered over the savannah in a life-like mural. It covered the entire wall, but the second giraffe hid behind a shelf of books, only his head visible. A group of children crowded around a table, shaking gourd rattles and playing African hand harps, while their parents shopped.

Beth found books ranging from those for the very young to young adult. Some books were so beautifully illustrated they could easily have been in the art section of the store.

Returning to the main area, she spotted Evelyn and Rosemary hovering by the punch bowl, their plates heaped with cookies and cake. Beth ducked down the health and self-help aisle, hoping to avoid an encounter. *What am I hiding for? It's my parents' store,* she thought. She hid anyway.

A book title caught her attention, *Schizophrenia, Early Intervention.* Her mind went back to something she had overhead her mother say, and she lifted the book from the shelf. Flipping to the table of contents, she found what she was looking for and opened to the chapter on symptoms.

Beth knew a lot of big words, but most of the page was beyond her. "Haal-oos-in-ation hallucination." She sounded out the word. "Sees or hears things that are not there." She slammed the book. *How could Mom think that? She's wrong. It was real.* Her own family didn't believe her and that stung.

But she began to see the danger of her situation. If she continued to insist that she could see what others could not, they would think she was sick. And then it hit her. *What if I am sick? What if none of it is real? . . . No, I'm not sick. I'm fine. I feel fine.*

The crowd thinned and Beth wandered up and down the aisles waiting for her parents to finish up and close the store. In the occult section, she was surprised to find several books written about fairies. One, *The Magic of Findhorn,* was an account of people who had dealings with fairies and lived in a rugged area of Scotland.

The store carries books deciding that people who "see things" are sick, while other books say there are fairies. This is lame, she thought. *It's completely opposite.* Beth decided, for her own peace of mind, to choose the fairy side of the question. And just to play it safe, from now on, she'd keep quiet about anything out of the ordinary. If she saw something, she would keep it to herself.

"Findhorn." Evelyn Chainy read over her shoulder. "What's

this?" She grabbed the book and glanced inside. "Beth's a little fairy girl. Maybe you should go to the children's section." Beth turned to walk away, but Rosemary blocked her escape. "Yeah, fairy girl."

She turned back to Evelyn, ready for an argument. Instead, she laughed, a great big belly laugh. "Who needs to go to the children's section?" Beth pointed. "You need your mommy to wipe the chocolate off your mouth."

Evelyn's eyes widened with surprise, and the blood rushed to her face. She whirled on Rosemary. "Why didn't you tell me?"

Rosemary whined and took a step back. "I didn't see it, honest."

Beth edged around them and walked away, the squabble behind her a perfect ending to the evening.

Chapter Twenty-six

A Guided Tour

Maeve sat at one of the long tables, sipping tea and poking at a bowl of thick porridge with her spoon. Scattered throughout the hall, a dozen imps quietly ate their breakfast. Nearly a week had gone by since her audience with the king and queen. Time passed slowly. She missed the everyday routine of friends and conversation. The imps, though polite, did little to make her feel welcome.

Bracken, the imp who had "escorted" her to the king's hall, walked by, carrying a large plate of food. *At least there's a familiar face,* she thought, looking his way. "Good morning," she said.

With no expression, Bracken nodded, choosing a seat farther on.

"Don't mind him," said an imp sitting nearby, "He's always like that." The imp stood and slid her bowl along the table, seating herself across from Maeve. "Always self-important," she whispered, tilting her head in his direction. She raised her eyebrows and folded her mouth in an accurate parody of Bracken, then burst into laughter.

So out of keeping was this gesture that Maeve's jaw dropped with surprise.

"My name is Aster." The imp reached across and grasped Maeve's hand in a vigorous shake.

"I'm Maeve." She nodded to the imp.

"It took a lot of backbone to come here and petition the king and queen," Aster said. "They're not often disposed to helping outsiders. And word has it that you have brought a rare and wondrous gift."

"It's a reflecting glass. It shows a clear image when you look into it."

"Ah," Aster said, "such a gift would delight the queen."

They ate their porridge for a while, in companionable silence. "Tell me, Maeve, what do you think of our home?" Aster asked, looking up from her bowl.

It's cold, dark, uninviting, and lonely, Maeve thought. "I really haven't seen much as yet," Maeve began, looking for the right words. "The hall is very large . . . and beautiful," she added, hastily.

Aster smiled. "There's much to see. When I've finished work, I'll come back and give you a tour."

Maeve brightened. "I would like that. What sort of work do you do?"

"I supervise the kennels. We'll go there first and you can see my little darlings. Be ready after the midday meal."

Looking ahead, Maeve saw only darkness. Dank air carried a taint of decay and set her stomach churning.

"This is it." Aster said, raising the light basket high.

No surprise there, Maeve thought, trying to adjust to the smell.

"Follow me." Aster took the lead. "Here we have a collection of some of the rarest salamanders to be found anywhere."

"Why do you keep salamanders?"

"They're quite useful, and salamanders are the king's passion. Mine as well. Here, let me show you what we have."

In the greenish glow of the light, Maeve saw a number of large pens set against a rock wall, each separated by a reed fence.

"This first pen houses our red-backed salamanders. Not very exotic, to be sure, but they are loyal companions. You may have noticed a few in the hall. The king always has one or two lying at his feet."

Maeve peered into the gloom. "All I see is rock."

"It's possible that you won't see them right now. They sleep during the day. Come on. We'll have better luck with the mudpuppies."

A trickle of water snaked down the rock face, filling the next pen. The still, black water showed no sign of inhabitants. *They must be sleeping too,* Maeve thought.

The blunt head of a mudpuppy burst through the water, closing in on Maeve with astonishing speed. She froze in horror, vaguely aware of a hand clamping onto her shoulder.

"Be careful, this one bites," Aster said, yanking her back.

With its quarry out of reach, the mudpuppy settled back in the water, its unblinking eyes focused intently.

Maeve shuddered and stepped farther away, not quite believing how close she had been to becoming salamander food. She turned to Aster. "It moved so fast."

Now, stretching over the water, the motionless body belied its watchful alertness. Dark blue spots covered its brown body, and brilliant red gills fanned feather-like from its neck.

"It puts me in mind of an ancient dragon," Maeve said, "but why would you keep such a creature? What possible use could it have?"

"Fishing. They hunt fish for us, and great sport it is. We let them loose in the pond, and they catch small fish and tadpoles." Aster caught the look of doubt on Maeve's face. "Really. It takes considerable training, and they only bring back a catch after their own bellies are full. Because of their size, it takes two imps to handle them. We swim them in a harness with a long rope. Swimming the mudpuppies is a popular outing, and many imps bring food and drink, sitting on the bank to enjoy the sport."

Aster guided Maeve to a second pool. "Over here we have a pair of waterdogs. They are similar to mudpuppies and used for fishing, but these also catch crayfish. You won't see them now. They are guarding a clutch of eggs just below the surface."

The salamander kennel was fascinating, and Maeve forgot, or adjusted to, the foul air. They came to a cave opening, blocked by a gate. Aster moved to open it.

"It's all right," she said, "These salamanders are harmless. Follow me."

Aside from their feet along the cave floor, only the faint sound of water could be heard. The walls of the cave closed in. The ceiling dropped and Aster stooped, bending at the waist to continue. The glow of the light basket offered little comfort, and Maeve wished that the tour would end.

The plop, plop of dripping water grew steadily louder, and before long, they came to a subterranean pool. Only the steady drops of condensation disturbed the still water.

"We'll wait here." Aster set her lamp on the floor and sat facing the pool.

A ripple appeared, followed by another. Emerging from the black water, a white, ghostly creature drew itself onto the bank.

Maeve caught her breath in wonder, "What an exquisite creature."

"Our living jewels," Aster said, smiling affectionately at the salamander. She drew an unsavory scrap from her bag and held it out.

Tadpole, Maeve thought.

The little beast turned toward the offering. Its head swayed back and forth catching the scent.

"It has no eyes," Maeve said with surprise.

Two tiny black dots, where the eyes should be, were buried below the skin. So delicate was the white hide, that it appeared almost transparent. In striking contrast, crimson gills stood out in long feathery plumes. Unerringly, the salamander reached the tadpole scrap, pulling it gently from Aster's hand. When it finished, it nudged the bag for more.

Maeve reached out and stroked the little head. It leaned into her touch, placing its foot on her knee.

"How soft," Maeve exclaimed. "What do you do with these creatures?"

"Their only function is their beauty, much like a flower."

Maeve began to see the imps in a different light. In spite of their differences, they shared a deep appreciation for beauty. "Are there very many of these creatures?" she asked, thoroughly charmed.

"It's hard to say. We never see more than a few at a time. They live deep in the water. It's so dark there that they have no need for eyes. They are called 'blind cave dwellers.'"

Aster stood. "There is something else I'd like to show you. Let's go back out." Giving the salamander a final pat, they walked back through the cave. The salamander followed them for a short distance, and then dropped back into the darkness.

Returning to the main part of the kennel, they followed along the rock wall, leaving the enclosures behind. The air grew warmer and dryer. It took a few moments for Maeve to realize that the light was not coming from Aster's basket. An orange glow illuminated the cave walls.

Aster set down her light. "No need for this," she said, and they continued on. The light and heat intensified. Soon the heat became uncomfortable. Hot air prickled at Maeve's nose, and she looked questioningly at Aster.

"Not much farther," was all she said.

Not much farther indeed, Maeve thought. *If we go much farther, we're going to incinerate.* She covered her face with her hands to block the heat.

"The salamanders are around the corner," Aster said, covering her face as well.

"This is close enough for me," Maeve gasped.

"Instead of rounding the corner," Aster said, "we'll walk to the far wall. We'll be able to see, and we'll be far enough away from the heat."

The heat-saturated ground smoldered under their feet, and hopping from one foot to the other, they moved swiftly to the back wall.

Turning, Aster gestured back toward the light. "Behold the fire beings."

Maeve cried out in astonishment. "Fire beings!" She squinted at a cleft in the rock where light spun in a vortex of liquid fire. Salamanders moved within, bodies of burnished copper against the white heat.

She knew the legend of these creatures: living in fire, impervious to flames, ancestor of ancient dragons. Nothing could have prepared Maeve for the vision before her. The movement of the salamanders appeared to determine the intensity of the heat. They dipped and swirled in unison so fast, that they seemed like a moving chain of copper. Slowing, they separated in graceful turns. White heat gave way to glowing red. The copper beasts darkened to black, silhouetted patterns against the brilliant flame.

"The Fire Dance," Maeve whispered, enthralled. "How is this

possible? From the old tales, they appear."

"The fire beings were here long before the imps," Aster said, "and we've learned little more than what you see now. The mystery heightens their beauty, does it not?"

Maeve turned to Aster. "Surely you don't use these creatures for anything, do you?"

"Come Maeve, we are a practical race."

"But using animals is such a human trait."

"Our relationship with the salamanders is one of greatest respect, as the fairies have with the plant kingdom."

"Tell me what the fire beings do?"

"Nothing. We leave them alone. There are, however, many tunnels branching out from their cave. One goes directly to the kitchen behind the hall for heating food, another to the garden."

"You have a garden?" Maeve's heart quickened.

"We do, but it isn't like the gardens you're used to."

"I'd love to see it," Maeve said. "Can we?"

"I'll have to ask the king for permission. There are secrets there that he may not be willing to share."

Chapter Twenty-seven

An Important Discovery

Strega and Rill lounged on the sofa, in the dark house. Beams of light through the window pinpointed them for an instant, then moved on as the family car slid into the driveway. The front door sprang open with a chorus of excited chatter.

"What a night," Steven Brinson, flung his coat over the arm of a chair, and sank gratefully into its soft cushion. "Could you believe the crowd in there? We sold so many books."

"It was our grand opening," his wife said. "I don't expect we'll be selling those quantities tomorrow."

"Come on, Annie, let me enjoy the moment." He smiled, kicked off his shoes and plunked his feet onto the coffee table.

Beth and Chris carried two boxes with leftover cakes and cookies directly into the kitchen. "We'll put them in the freezer," their mother said, joining them. "They'll be great to pack in your lunches for the next ten years or so."

"Not in my lunch," Chris said. "I don't want to look at another cookie."

"You'll change your mind by tomorrow, count on it." Beth said, with a jaw-splitting yawn. "I'm off to bed. Goodnight." She left her Mom and Chris to finish up in the kitchen and went into the living room to say goodnight to her Dad.

The smell tipped her off, and her heart clenched. The decision not to react in front of her family was being put to the test sooner, rather than later. She gritted her teeth, raised her chin, and walked directly in front of the sofa. Stinking, vaporous forms sprawled on the cushions. Their malevolent eyes bored into hers, then widened with surprise when she pulled up an old rocking chair and seated herself.

She rocked casually and without concern. "That was fun, Dad," she said, with a bright smile. "You and Mom did an awesome job on the bookstore. Everyone was talking about how great it looked, especially the children's section."

"Thanks, Beth, I'm glad you enjoyed yourself. We really appreciated the help tonight. You and Chris did a terrific job."

She stole a glance at the sofa. They hadn't moved, but to her surprise she could barely see them and the smell was gone. Turning back to her Dad, she flashed a brilliant smile, and from the corner of her eye saw the creatures dissolve to nothing more than a wisp.

Beth felt strong. For the first time in weeks, she felt in control. She saw how her actions affected the creatures, and ignoring them seemed to be the best solution. If they ever returned, there would be no freaking out; she'd just go about her business. "Goodnight, Dad." She rose and kissed him. Walking up the stairs, she never looked back to see if the unwanted guests had gone.

"She saw us. I know she saw us." Rill craned his neck around and watched Beth walk away.

"We can't use her anymore." Strega said.

"Then we should move on, try someone else." Rill insisted, frustrated with their failure. "We've wasted enough time."

"Do you question my methods?" Strega growled.

"No." Rill took a hasty step back.

"Let me lay it out for you. The portal will be secured for the solstice assault. The wiggin invasion is in place. Everything hinges on our success, and I see no obstacles."

"But how do you expect to reopen the portal?" Rill looked doubtful.

"The fairies don't pose a threat, and their precious light grows weaker."

"She's not that weak," Rill grumbled. "She closed the portal behind us, and now we're stuck here."

Strega put an arm over Rill's shoulders with a surprising show of patience. "Look at this as an opportunity."

"I can't see it. We have no real power here."

"Oh, but we do have power, Rill. We have influence. We have manipulation. All we need to complete our assignment is one angry human."

The wiggins followed Beth to school, taking great care to stay out of sight. After several days they felt disheartened. No one they had come across would serve their purposes.

"I have to admit that my impression of humans is flawed," Strega said. "Many people have some anger, but it's only a small portion of their other emotions. Most of it we can't use."

"We should look for someone older," Rill suggested. "Most of the people here are children."

"I had hoped to find someone who knows Beth. It would be easier to put our defenses in place, in case Beth decides to protect the land. We'll give it a little longer, and if we don't find someone suitable, we'll move on."

Beth entered the hall from her classroom, and the wiggins ducked into an alcove for cover, watching her from the shadows. She pushed through another door and after a few minutes came out again, heading back to her classroom.

Just before she reached the door, it opened and a tall girl walked toward her. Beth began to walk around, but the girl blocked her way.

"What's your problem, Evelyn?"

"I don't like your smart mouth, and you dress like Farmer MacGreggor."

"That's stupid," Beth said looking down at her jeans and sneakers. "And you look like a music video reject."

"There goes that mouth of yours." Evelyn moved closer.

Beth quickly darted around, but Evelyn caught a fistful of her sleeve.

"Just so you know," Evelyn said, pulling Beth close, "if I see you alone and away from school, you'd better run."

Beth jerked her arm free and stalked back to class.

"Evelyn." Strega said with delight. "Yes, Evelyn will do nicely."

The small, yellow house spoke of emptiness. Dark drapes drew across the front windows. When Evelyn climbed onto the porch, she kicked a stack of newspapers out of the way, not minding when some fluttered down into the yard. The wiggins followed her inside.

A woman lay asleep on the sofa. An empty bag of potato chips rested on her chest, rising and falling with her snores. Daytime TV blared. Empty bottles and an ashtray, filled to brimming, cluttered the coffee table. Chip crumbs littered the floor, and one small fragment stuck to the edge of her mouth.

Evelyn pressed her lips in a frown. She turned off the TV, cleared and wiped the table, and went into the kitchen to prepare dinner: boxed macaroni and cheese.

"Wake up." Evelyn removed the chip bag, replacing it with a bowl of orange cheesy pasta.

"I don't want any," her mother said, turning her head away. "I'm sick of it."

"This is what I know how to make. Instead of complaining, why don't you cook something?"

Her mother sat up, eyes moist with impending tears. "Don't be angry, Evie."

"Are you going to cry again?" Evelyn grabbed the remote, turned on the TV, and threw herself into a chair. She ignored her mother, flicking from one channel to another, while her mother wept quietly.

"It would do you good to cry." Her mother wiped her eyes and blew into a tissue. "Your father died, and you didn't shed a single tear."

"Leave me alone." Evelyn exploded, snapped up her bowl, and stormed from the room.

She sat on her bed in the deepening shadows, her meal untouched. *I don't need to cry,* she thought. Her mother had cried enough for the both of them.

After the funeral, Evelyn found herself becoming the mother, and her mother just crumpled up. "Depression," the doctor had said, prescribing medicine. "Your mother needs some time to grieve." Evelyn waited almost a year, and she'd had enough. Time was up. Her fists squeezed. She just wanted to smash something, anything. After a while her thudding heart settled to a normal pace, but the night grew old before she could drop off to sleep.

"Our schedule has taken a soaring leap forward," Strega said, watching Evelyn sleep. "We'll set up in the house and plan our next move. For the most effective sendings, we should study this girl carefully."

"How much control can we expect?" Rill asked.

"If done properly, quite a lot. We'll color her thoughts and build on her existing attitude."

"If we aren't careful with our sendings, she'll be able to see everything: the fairies, the light, even us." Rill frowned. "I'm not sure about this."

"Not to worry. That's where influence and manipulation come in. Influence and manipulation, Rill, two powerful tools. If she comes across the fairies she'll find them repulsive little maggots, and when we come into view she'll believe she is blessed with guardian angels."

"What of the portal? Can she open it for us?" Rill gestured to Evelyn with a lift of his chin.

"She has one task only and that is to cut down the birch tree."

"Aren't you forgetting the fairies and Beth? You know they won't sit by and let that happen."

Strega's eyes gleamed. "It's simple. We kill them. Or should I say Evelyn will kill them."

Chapter Twenty-eight

Breach of Trust

Time exhaled in a long, boring breath. The weeks melted into one another, and Maeve had never known such dreariness. *Fairies are not cut out for caves,* she thought on a particularly tiresome day. *How can the imps live like this?* She longed for sun and air.

Her thoughts turned to the imp garden. *For plants to grow, there has to be an opening to the outside,* she reasoned. With each passing day, the garden had taken on more fantastic proportions. Maeve imagined huge exotic flowers of every color, the air sweet with fragrance. Even trees grew in this garden, lifting their branches to greet the light, streaming in from above.

Why had Aster even mentioned the garden if she wasn't allowed to see it? The king had declared it "Off limits."

"Not all imps can access the garden," Aster had explained. "It's a privilege accorded to those the king deems worthy. I'm sorry, Maeve."

Weeks later, Maeve still bristled at the slight. *What's the matter with him? Is he afraid I'll steal his vegetables, pick his flowers? I'm a fairy. I belong in a garden.*

Maeve sat alone, listlessly munching cattail pollen bread. Its unique flavor had lost its appeal over the weeks. Bits of conversation reached her from imps seated throughout the hall. In this way, she gathered any snippets of news, helping to break the monotony of the long day.

"Garden," someone said above the hum of voices.

Maeve held her breath, straining to catch the words.

"Let's go after we've finished," an imp said to his friend.

She waited, thinking of all the reasons why she should not go against the king's wishes, but reason fled. When the imps left the hall, she followed them into a wide tunnel.

This is a serious breach of trust, she thought, but she continued trailing the imps. *I won't go in. I'll just see where it is.*

Carefully, she followed, sinking into darkened doorways when other imps came into view. Under her breath, she counted the passages. "One right, two left, two right." Maeve realized that the return would be backwards, and felt a moment of panic trying to get the sequence straight.

They stopped in front of large wooden doors, beautifully carved with the sun, the moon, and stars, above a geometric pattern of cubes and hexagonal shapes. Before entering the garden, one of the imps paused, as if sensing Maeve's presence. He turned and, narrowing his eyes, checked the gloomy corridor.

She pressed herself into the darkest shadows, grateful that the light baskets were set at such long intervals. Maeve felt sure that she wouldn't be seen, but the possibility made her weak in the knees. *I'm going back,* she decided. She wasn't going in anyway.

The door opened. Maeve's eyes widened, transfixed, as a radiant stream of light fell upon the imps. They stood, poised on the threshold of ordinary and otherworldly. And then they vanished through the door, leaving Maeve alone in the gloom.

I knew it! There is an opening to the outside, she thought with a thrill. That brief glimpse set in Maeve a relentless longing. She knew that she would return.

Drawing the curtain aside, Maeve checked the corridor for signs of life. No one stirred. She cautiously eased out of her chamber. It occurred to her that imps might be on watch in the main hall. She chose a smaller tunnel, which she knew would skirt the hall and link her with the appropriate tunnel to the garden.

"One right, two left, two right," she intoned. Although she felt sure that most imps slept, her heart raced. She remained alert for any movement or sound, her own feet silent upon the earthen floor. Arriving at the tall wooden doors, she paused, struck by the richness of the polished wood. She ran an appreciative hand over the carving of the sun, and then pushed.

Maeve found absolute darkness; no light baskets, no moonlight. With extended hands, she felt along the wall, finding a suitable place to sit and wait for sunrise. Moist air carried a freshness she had not enjoyed since arriving at the imp kingdom. She smiled, breathing deeply. *The air alone is enough to take this risk,* she thought. With a few hours remaining until sunrise, she felt it would be safe to close her eyes and sleep.

Sunlight stroked her cheek. Maeve stirred, and remembering where she was, opened her eyes to view the garden. She gasped with astonishment. The amber light of morning ignited thousands of crystals, and the air shimmered with rainbows. The cavern was an enormous geode, no flowers or plants to be found.

"It's a crystal garden," she whispered, hardly believing what unfolded before her. As the sun continued to rise, the light fell upon more crystals, releasing their rainbows to dance among the others. Soon the cavern swirled with light and color.

A narrow path wound through crystals of every hue. Reminded of flowerbeds, she stopped to admire a thicket of violet amethyst. Farther along lay a carpet of opals, colors igniting from their fiery depths. In all directions light sparkled and bounced.

She knew that she should leave and had made up her mind to do so, when she noticed soft tendrils of mist curling along the path. *A few more minutes won't hurt,* she decided, and continued on. The mist thickened, swirling about her ankles, and soon she came to a pool. Only glimpses of the water could be seen through the mist. She touched the surface with her foot, pulling back with surprise. It was hot!

I could swim and still get back without being discovered, provided that I mind the time, she thought. Wading into the water, savoring the warmth, she lay with arms outstretched, sinking below the mist. The sun shone fully through the cavern opening, transforming the mist to creamy fog. She could see nothing and was content to float, cocooned in liquid and light. Time and purpose withdrew, and she surrendered to silence.

Is the water getting hotter? No, I've become overheated, she realized with a jolt. She'd been in the water far too long. Swimming to the pool's edge, she pulled herself out, red-faced and dizzy.

Maeve tottered up the path, determined to reach the shadow of the tunnels before she was discovered. *What if the tunnels are full of imps already? I'm wringing wet. How will I explain that?*

These worries were replaced by a much larger problem. When she pushed through the door, she smacked headlong into the worst possible imp.

Caught off guard, Bracken frowned at Maeve, considering what it was that seemed so out of place. Soon an unpleasant smile crossed his lips. "Your name is not on the list for garden visits."

Maeve thought of darting around him, but his looming figure left no avenue for escape.

As though sensing her thoughts, his smile broadened. "The queen should be informed of your conduct. The king is gone until tomorrow, and this transgression deserves immediate attention." The familiar grip clamped on her shoulder. "Now move."

"The queen?" Maeve squeaked. Even through the redness of her overheated body, her face blanched.

The tunnel bustled with imps, and they glanced curiously at Maeve. Some turned to follow, hoping for a bit of entertainment. She trotted beside Bracken's long strides, her mind racing with possible excuses. There were no excuses for betraying the laws of hospitality.

The number of imps who followed swelled to a raucous crowd, and she knew that her shame would become a public affair. Already the hall was filling, and the imps parted as Bracken propelled her forward to stand before the queen. Maeve bowed low, painfully aware of the water dripping from her garments onto the woven carpet.

The queen leaned forward in her chair. "I wasn't aware that you had received an invitation to the garden."

"No, your majesty."

"And did you enjoy your visit? The crystals are magnificent, are they not?" The queen continued conversationally, almost pleasantly.

"Yes, your majesty, the garden was very beautiful."

The queen bolted from her chair. "See what she has stolen!"

Leaping back in alarm, Maeve collided with Bracken, who grabbed onto her in a tight grip.

"Please, I would never . . ."

"Silence!"

As Bracken checked her clothes, Mauve stood rigid, stabbed intermittently by indignation and shame.

"Nothing," Bracken declared.

"Could she have dropped some crystals in the tunnels?" the queen asked.

"Unlikely," Bracken replied.

The hall hummed with speculation, and the imps eagerly awaited the queen's decree. There was very little crime in the imp community, as their mischievous nature was usually satisfied with raids into neighboring kingdoms. Maeve's actions caused quite a stir.

The queen returned to her chair. "Fortunately for you, you are not a thief. But you have blatantly disregarded the laws of hospitality. Why would you do this?"

"I wanted to see the sun," Maeve stammered.

A ripple of laughter moved through the hall.

"I wanted to see the sun," The queen mocked. "I order you to remain in your quarters for the duration of your stay, at which time I will take great pleasure in the ruin of your fairy celebration. And don't bother trying to sneak out," she added. "The door will be guarded. Take her away."

Amidst a jeering crowd, Bracken removed Maeve from the hall in disgrace. The short walk to her quarters felt endless, bombarded with the shouts and snipes of a following crowd. When the chamber curtain fell behind her, she welcomed the silence.

Chapter Twenty-nine

The Garden Emporium

The weather is warming up. I think it's time to plant something," Beth said to her mother.

"What have you got in mind?"

"I'm not sure. Mrs. Peasgood told me about the perennials already growing like irises and tulips. But I want to plant other flowers."

"You mean annuals?" Beth gave her a blank look. "Plants that you put in the ground every year."

"Yes, annuals."

"I'm driving to town for groceries and to pick up your dad after work. Why don't you come along, and we'll stop at the garden center."

"DeForest Garden Emporium." Beth read the sign as they pulled in. Attached to the main building were two large greenhouses. Bordering the parking lot stood rows of potted shrubs and fruit trees.

Through the doors, the air held the earthy scent of growing things. Beth felt enlivened, as if each breath contained spring itself. She headed straight for the greenhouses, finding row upon row of colorful flowers.

"Do we have to buy seeds? Couldn't we buy some of these flowers?"

"It's hard to resist," her mother said, "but there is plenty of time to plant seeds, and you'll have more flowers if you grow them yourself."

A man looked up from a thatch of green foliage and waved. "Be right with you," he called. Returning to his work, he hummed a spirited bit of opera, his plant sprayer spritzing in perfect rhythm. When he completed the job, he blotted his forehead with a handkerchief, which he pulled from one of his over-stuffed pockets.

Beth noticed an array of articles hanging in and around each pocket. Partially visible were keys on a chain, plant clippers, an ink pen, a small notebook, a wallet, and a small bottle of sunscreen. His pockets were so jam packed, the effect was much like a gopher's cheeks filled to capacity.

"I believe we've met before," the man said. "It was at the bookstore opening. Am I right?"

"You are. I'm Anne Brinson. This is my daughter, Beth."

"Yes, you served punch and cookies. I remember. I'm Bob DeForest. I have to say that I was mightily impressed with the books you carry on gardening."

"Thank you," Beth's mother said.

"What can I do for you today?"

"I made a list of seeds I'd like to buy," Beth said, handing the list to Bob. "I have a twenty-five dollar budget."

"Let me see here." Bob slipped on his reading glasses, which hung from a string around his neck. I think we can outfit you with everything you'll need to get started.

Bob proved to be full of useful information. He asked questions about where Beth intended to plant and indicated which flowers liked sun or shade "A neglected garden? Have you given thought to fertilizer?" he asked, piling the seeds on the counter. "It sounds like the soil will need a nutritional boost."

Beth wasn't sure what to say or what questions to ask.

"When you are ready to fertilize, come and see me." He gestured expansively to a corner of the greenhouse, stacked high with boxes and bags. "We have your 10-10-5, your 5-15-20, your 20-20-20 . . ."

She stared at the assortment of fertilizers in bewilderment as he rattled off half a dozen possibilities.

"All very scientific," he added, noticing her confusion.

"I had no idea how much you have to know to be a gardener," Beth said to her mother when they drove away.

"Don't worry. You'll do fine, and you'll learn a lot as you go along."

Beth didn't look convinced.

"Tell you what, when I'm working at the bookstore, I'll take a peek at some of those gardening books. See what I can find out."

The earthy smell and moist texture of the soil felt good in Beth's hands. She filled little peat pots and pushed a seed into each one. The simple act of planting felt as though she'd done it all her life.

Bob DeForest suggested peat pots. Beth could plant them directly in the ground, without disturbing the tiny roots. She put them on a tray and claimed the kitchen window for her mini-garden.

Her mother came home with fertilizing information. "For starters, the flowerbeds should be turned over and the dirt loosened." She explained, handing Beth a list of instructions. "Then you can work the fertilizer into the soil."

"Thanks for looking this stuff up, Mom." She took the paper and scanned down the list.

"You know, this is a pretty big job. Are you certain that you're not taking on too much?"

"Don't worry. I'll do a little each day after school. That way the work won't seem so hard. And hey," Beth smiled, "I can quit whenever I want."

The garden plan that she and Mrs. Peasgood had drawn came in handy. Grass had grown in thick mats, covering all the flowerbeds. Without the plan, Beth wouldn't have known where to dig.

Taking on this project—her own project—excited Beth. She dug up the sod, a little each day after school. To her surprise, at the end of her digging session, she pushed through the kitchen door dirty and hungry, but also energized.

Chapter Thirty

Unexpected Visitor

At twilight, by the stone steps, Beth shifted from one foot to the other. She cleared her throat and leaned self-consciously over a patch of tulips. "I'm going to fertilize the garden," she announced in a hushed tone. Clearly, her message needed to be louder. Glancing shyly around the yard, she checked to see if anyone was watching. Cupping her mouth with her hands, she shouted, "I'm going to fertilize the garden," and hurried away.

I did it, she thought, feeling a blush settle on her cheeks. It felt silly shouting like that. *What if the fairies aren't even there?*

When she reached the porch steps, darkness had settled in, and the rising moon edged the top of the trees. The welcoming scent of dinner greeted her at the door, and her stomach responded with a hungry rumble.

The house lay beneath a full moon, gilded with light. Within, all were asleep except Beth, who lay quietly, watching the cast of light and shadow across the floor. The night wore on and sleep remained elusive. Sighing heavily, she tossed back the covers and rose to open the window. Instantly the night air flowed in, filling the room with freshness.

It must be late by now, she thought. A glance at the clock confirmed it, and she groaned. Without sleep, school would be miserable in the morning. Climbing back into bed, she fluffed the pillow and pulled the blankets to her chin.

Later, she heard her name through foggy layers of sleep. Trying to focus, she opened her eyes with difficulty.

The moon shone fully through her window, silver streaming

upon her bed like a celestial spotlight. In that spotlight, only inches from her nose, a small figure stood squarely on her pillow. She bolted upright, knocking over a cup of water from the nightstand in her haste. The fairy leaped nimbly to the blanket and waited.

"Thornby, what are you doing here?"

"You opened the window, and I wanted to discuss your plans for fertilizing the garden."

She gave him a puzzled look. "I can see you perfectly. You're not blinking in and out."

"That's because you're helping me. Your mind no longer questions what your eyes tell you."

"Because I believe in fairies?" Clapping for Tinker Bell came to mind.

"Yes. It's doubt that gets in the way. Now tell me, what fertilizer do you intend to use?"

"I don't know yet. I guess I'll buy something at the garden center in town."

Thornby clasped his hands behind his back and padded across the blanket. "Let's keep it simple. Use well-rotted manure, horse or cow is fine. Later you can look into composting."

"Composting?"

"Don't worry about that now." Turning around, he paced back the other way, leaving tiny dimples in the blanket. As he walked, Beth took a moment to study him.

To her delight, she saw that he did indeed have pointy ears. He wore a belted tunic, which hung to his knees, and leggings. In the moonlight, it was difficult to make out the color. *Earthy tones*, Beth decided. Even if fairies were visible to most humans, they'd be difficult to spot, blending right in with the foliage.

Thornby hopped back onto her pillow, again startling her with his quick movements.

"When do you intend to fertilize?" he asked.

"I have to get the fertilizer first, and I need time to prepare the soil. I can probably do it in a few weeks."

"That will be fine. There is a tangled bit of garden to the left of the birches, no need to fertilize that area. That is where we will stay until the manure has settled into the ground."

"Now I see why you need to know my plans," Beth laughed. "Getting caught under a load of manure would be terrible. You'd have to dig your way out."

"Yes it would be terrible," Thornby said, stiffly.

Beth stifled her laugh to a giggle. "Sorry, I guess that's not funny."

"That's all right. Being buried in manure may sound funny, but it's one experience I wish to avoid."

Beth wondered if perhaps he had already experienced that, or some equally disastrous blunder by unknowing humans.

Their business concluded and Thornby seemed ready to leave, but Beth had questions that needed answers.

"I have seen something terrible lately. I don't know what they are, except that they're nasty and smell bad, like something dead."

Thornby looked troubled and stood silent for a moment. "They call themselves wiggins. We were alarmed when they first appeared, then realized that they had no power. They get their strength from negativity, anger, or fear. The fairies gave them nothing. We thought they had moved on, but they must have moved into the house."

Beth pointed to the attic. "Only I could see them. They scared me so badly that my parents thought I was sick. But the last time I saw them, I ignored them, so my parents wouldn't get upset. I pretended they weren't there."

"And what happened?"

"They disappeared. I think they're gone."

"I believe they have, but they are worrisome, nonetheless. Given the right circumstances, they can certainly cause trouble."

"What do they want?"

"They find this world appealing and want to call it home, bringing their race here to settle."

Beth looked stricken.

"There's no need to worry. The entrance they used is closed and well guarded. They will not succeed. What we are looking at here are two desperate wiggins, who can't return home."

"Why do they change from a mist to a solid?"

"Anger and fear. They feed on it, and it makes them whole but never permanently. Taking solid form is what attracts them to this world. They have been able to eat and taste. It's a new experience and they like it. Hopefully, we've seen the last of them."

"Tell me about the light I saw in the birches."

Thornby smiled. "Rest well." He gave a short bow and hopped off the pillow onto the floor, then easily to the windowsill.

To Beth's delight, conversing late into the night with a fairy felt perfectly natural. She waved as he disappeared through the window.

Over the next few weeks, for an hour after school and on weekends, Beth prepared the flowerbeds. She removed the sod, turned the soil, and finished off by adding the fertilizer. On Mrs. Peasgood's advice, she cut back the rose bushes and fertilized them as well.

Many seasonal flowers, such as iris and tiger lilies, grew among clumps of weeds. With these, she separated the tangled roots, giving them room to grow, and weeded as best she could. The extra roots she transferred to other areas.

Beth placed the seedlings into the freshly turned dirt, feeling deeply satisfied when she stepped back to view the results.

Thornby did not visit again, nor did she spot any other fairies. But by the end of May, the flowers proclaimed fairy influence, by blooming early and brightly in all the beds. Aside from watering and a bit of weeding, Beth felt that she was finished, at least for this year.

Her parents expressed their surprise that Beth would take on a project this big and actually finish it. She hadn't displayed that kind of staying power in the past. Both agreed that their little girl was "growing up." Beth just smiled, thinking that a five-inch fairy can be a great motivator.

Chapter Thirty-one

A Fine Temper

Ten steps from wall to wall." Maeve counted the dimensions of her cell, for her quarters had been transformed into a prison. Activity was limited to sitting, sleeping, and pacing. In her solitude, she took a long look at her difficulties.

What was she thinking to seek out the imps? Her decision was not about teaching the fairies a lesson, but really about her anger. She was startled to realize that she hadn't thought about her house for weeks and further surprised that she didn't care.

Maeve missed her friends and the garden, despite its run-down state. Thinking of the garden, the words of the queen struck a harsh chord. "I will take pleasure in the ruin of your fairy celebration."

What did that mean? The king and queen hadn't discussed their plans with Maeve. They assured her that they would look after the details. She paced another loop around the room, fretting at what she had started and could not stop.

"Hello, Maeve." Aster poked her head around the curtain. "Mind if I come in? I've brought you some supper."

Maeve had not seen Aster since the garden incident and felt unsure of her friend's feelings. "Please come in," she replied, hesitantly.

"Well, Maeve," Aster said, setting a tray on the table, "you've gone from honored guest to house arrest. You just couldn't resist a peek."

Maeve shifted uneasily, saying nothing.

"Curiosity, impulsiveness, and a fine temper. That's what I like about you, Maeve. You're just a short imp." Aster laughed.

This joke was unexpected, and Maeve's mouth dropped in surprise. Aster laughed harder, relishing her friend's bewilderment.

She fell onto the bench and pounded the table with a big guffaw.

This display burst the dam, and Maeve threw her head back and laughed.

Aster drew in some air and dabbed her eyes with her sleeve, before she could master the art of speech. "I needed a good laugh and by the looks of it, so did you. Any imp would have done the same thing in your position. The trick is to not get caught."

"I was sure that you would be angry with me," Maeve said.

"Not at all. But what I can't understand is why you stayed so long. Couldn't you have taken just a quick look?"

"That was the plan," Maeve said, seating herself across from Aster, "until I found the hot-water pool. The hot water, the crystals, the rainbows; I've never seen anything like it. Does the hot water come from the fire beings?"

"It does. Actually, the fire beings are responsible for the entire garden. Ages ago, their liquid fire blended with minerals in the cave. When the mixture cooled, the crystals formed. Of course that was long before the imps arrived."

"Do the fire beings make liquid fire?"

"I think they are liquid fire. Many imps feel that the salamanders are the very essence of fire. When they spin the flames, dancing and swirling, we believe it is an expression of play."

"I don't understand."

"No one does. The Fire Dance creates more than a variation in temperature. When you watch, you can feel heat growing within you, and your own rhythms fall into harmony with the dance." Aster's eyes shone with passion. "It's a celebration. Perhaps the fire is celebrating itself. Who knows? The mystery is also a treasure. It has inspired countless poems and songs, and is the basis of our long love of salamanders."

"You imps have a rich culture," Maeve admitted, with growing respect. "It takes so many directions. Imps seem to be, first and foremost, mischievous and even alarming. And yet there is great depth."

Aster inclined her head. "Thank you. Like our crystals, we are many faceted."

Maeve eyed the tray of food. "What did you bring?"

"Enough food for both of us. I thought you could use the company." Aster looked around the sparse chamber. "There's not a lot for you to do."

"No, there isn't. I'm very restless."

"I hope this helps." Aster pushed a lidded clay bowl toward Maeve, "Fairy food."

Maeve removed the lid. "Wild strawberries!"

"And my favorite form of honey," Aster said, producing a flask and two cups, "mead."

Maeve's confinement had stretched from one tedious day to the next. Indeed, she had lost count of the days, the meals signaling morning and evening. Aster's visit by contrast, felt like a monumental event.

"Good news. The king and queen, along with a company of carefully chosen imps, will set out for your home in two days."

Maeve leaped from the table, shrieking with delight, and threw her arms around Aster, nearly knocking her from the bench.

Aster returned her hug. "I know you are eager to see your friends and homeland again."

Struck by the purpose of the journey, Maeve returned to her seat more sedately. "What plan is in place to disrupt the celebration?" she asked.

Aster studied her friend for a moment. "You no longer wish for revenge."

"No. I have had time to think. It's that 'fine temper' you spoke of that led me here. I fooled myself into believing that the fairies needed to be taught a lesson, when really, I wanted to satisfy my anger. I feel ashamed."

Aster shook her head. "I'm sorry. The consequences are unfolding. There is nothing you can do now."

"I know."

"And who knows what will happen. You'll just have to wait and see."

"Do you know what the king has in mind?"

"Aphids is what I heard, but I don't know the details."

Maeve winced. "How many aphids?"

"Really, I couldn't say. But I do know that many salamanders will be used to carry them. Our weavers have fashioned special baskets for the trip."

Aster pulled a small packet from her pocket and pushed it toward Maeve. "I wanted you to have this parting gift."

"You won't be coming?"

"No. My job is here with the remaining salamanders. Go ahead and open it." She nodded at the packet, covered in a brightly dyed cloth and tied with some marsh grass.

Maeve carefully unwrapped the small bundle revealing a rough piece of stone. Embedded in the underside lay a white milky gem. When she held it up for a closer look, the stone ignited in the glow of the light basket. Tiny flashes of orange and red glittered from below its murky sheath.

"It's a fire opal. I wanted you to have something to remember your garden adventure, my little sun seeker."

"You are a good friend, Aster. Thank you for your gift and your hospitality."

That night as Maeve lay in her bed a feeling of peace settled upon her, the first she had known for a long time. She abandoned the need to be in control and surrendered the future to what will be.

Chapter Thirty-two

Over the Edge

Rosemary sat on the toilet, in the stall farthest from the door, sobbing and blowing her nose on coarse toilet paper. When someone entered the bathroom, she stifled her crying and drew her feet up and out of sight. A girl knocked and pushed against the locked door, then moved on, deciding the toilet was out of order.

Alone again, her sobs echoed off the tiled walls, and tears streamed down her cheeks, soaking her shirt.

Evelyn had liked her. For Rosemary, a girl with little confidence, that meant something. She had felt accepted. Her sense of belonging, held firmly in place by Evelyn's friendship, lay shattered.

She couldn't go to class. She couldn't be seen in the hall. People would know that Evelyn had dumped her. What that meant unfolded for Rosemary with painful clarity. Her friendship with Evelyn excluded everyone else. (Not that it mattered.) No one liked her anyway. The bathroom door opened again, and someone settled in the next stall.

Rosemary wadded more paper, holding it against her mouth and nose. Evelyn's words played over in her mind. "Get out of my face and quit following me around. I don't like you any more." A sob escaped the muffle of paper.

"Hey, are you okay in there?"

"Fine," Rosemary sniffed.

"Is that you, Rosemary?" Beth asked, recognizing her voice. "Where's your buddy, Evelyn?"

That brought on a new wave of sobs. "She's changed. She doesn't want to hang around with me anymore."

"Seriously, that doesn't sound like a bad thing." Beth walked over to the sink to wash up.

Rosemary left the stall, encouraged by Beth's lack of gloating. She held paper against her running nose, and her red eyes looked away with embarrassment.

"It can't be that bad," Beth said, surprised at Rosemary's pain.

"It's worse. I think she's crazy. She told me that her new friends don't like me, and she went on about them being guardian angels and how special she was."

"Sounds like she's lost it all right." Beth washed her hands and headed for the bathroom door, not minding at all that Evelyn had gone over the edge. She couldn't help feeling sorry for Rosemary though. "Feel better," she said, and offered a smile.

"Wait. You don't get it. Evelyn's friends don't like me, but they hate you."

"Me? Why? I don't even know them." Beth threw up her hands. "More like guardian devils," she said with aggravation, and left the bathroom.

"Watch your back." She heard as the door closed behind her.

Chapter Thirty-three

Many Changes

The caravan wound through stands of trees and thick brush, picking its way along hidden paths. The king and queen led the procession in a brightly painted carriage, pulled by six mud puppies. Imps walked alongside, each carrying a bucket of water. Every so often, they doused the salamanders to keep them from drying out. A nearby water wagon provided fresh buckets, and a second team of imps replaced the first, so no one became overtired.

Maeve walked behind the carriage, flanked by two imp guards. Nearing three weeks, by her count, the tedious pace of the caravan sucked her patience dry. Why were they taking so long? She had made the same trip in three days.

For the imps, late afternoon and early evening proved the ideal time to travel, being cooler and easier on the salamanders. They stopped at dusk to settle in for the night, setting up tents and serving food. Light baskets, placed around the perimeter, attracted fireflies, which darted like shooting stars over the camp. Well into the night, the imps gathered for music and dance, passing around pitchers of mead. In the morning, they all slept late.

Certain chores had to be done before they could break camp. One job was to feed tender leaves to the aphids and make sure they still thrived. These green, pear-shaped insects, no larger than a sesame seed, had voracious appetites. In one day, they consumed enough sap to equal twice their weight.

It had been no small feat to collect the aphids, and quite a few imps had to be treated for ant bites. Ants and aphids can always be found together. Like humans with cows, ants milk aphids, extracting sweet nectar. And, like putting cows out to pasture, ants take their aphids to feed on plants, guarding them against predators. The imps collected enough aphids to damage at least two healthy rose bushes, an aphid's favorite food.

The caravan arrived at a field that Maeve knew well, situated west of the birches of her home. The imps decided the place was far enough away that the fairies were unlikely to discover their presence. They began unloading their supplies, setting up a more permanent camp.

Maeve asked if she could go home right then and there. The king refused, and she endured yet another night, sleeping in a guarded tent. In the morning, she was led before the king and queen.

They appeared to be quite at home, perched on the same thrones from the imp hall. Maeve saw that much of the trappings and splendor had been transported to their final camp, set under canopies. Carpets and wall hangings lent the appearance of gaiety to the otherwise stern leaders. The imps enjoyed their comfort.

"You may return to your home," the king said, "but do not betray us."

"Why would she?" the queen said. "If she tells the fairies what she has done, they will send her packing. No, I think our secret is safe."

"Bracken, Mugwort." the king motioned for two imps to approach. "Escort our guest back to her home, scout out the lay of the land, and then report back."

Maeve bowed, saying nothing (what could she say?) and was led away.

The sight of the birches swelled her heart. She hurried along the path, only to stop, open-mouthed, before a garden blazing with color. How she had missed this place, and how it had changed! Inhaling deeply, she gave herself over to the welcome scent of home.

The garden wasn't perfect, but it was certainly worthy of the midsummer celebration. Peonies, lilacs, and irises, called from every corner. They appeared every year, but until now had been sparse and pale. These blooms floated like colored ships on a sea of green.

The roses held mastery, with velvet petals of claret red, dew glistening from the darker folds. *They've been fertilized and pruned,* Maeve thought. Then she remembered the aphids and her heart ached.

"Maeve is back," came a shout. In no time the fairies crowded around, all talking at once. "Welcome back, Maeve." "Are you all right?" "Where have you been?"

More fairies poured out of the shrubs to join the growing crowd. Maeve was warmed by the welcome.

"It's good to see all of you," she said, "and the garden looks beautiful. Tell me what has been going on here."

"It's mostly Thornby's doing," Artemus said. "He met with one of the children and told her what we needed. As she worked in the garden, we did our part." He gestured to the glowing plants.

"So I see," Maeve said.

The fairies stood quietly, expectantly, waiting for Maeve to tell them where she had been. To avoid this subject, she hoisted her carry bag higher on her shoulder. "I suppose I'd better look for some lodging."

Everyone laughed.

"Come on, Maeve," Artemus said, "We'll help you find something."

Everyone laughed again.

"What's going on?" she asked, missing the joke.

"Nothing," they all chimed in.

They ushered her to a lilac bush, thick with purple flowers. Within, barely visible, Maeve saw a small door.

"Welcome to your new home!" The fairies cried in unison.

She stood stunned, unable to speak, at once grateful but feeling undeserving of such a gift.

"Well, come take a look," Thornby said, joining the group.

She smiled uncertainly and pushed on the door. A number of fairies detached themselves from the group and followed her inside.

All fairy entrances face east. To take advantage of that, an agate was set in the middle of the door, to glow softly in the morning's first light.

As with most bowers, the dwelling was woven of living branches. In this case, lilac constructed the basic tunnel. However, breaking with tradition, Maeve saw that the walls were multi-colored. She ran her fingers over the tight weave.

"This is remarkable," she said.

"It was Juniper's idea to weave the lilac with red willow," Thornby said, admiring the unique pattern.

A community effort, Maeve's home showed an abundance of creativity. Those who had not worked directly on the construction brought items to replace what was lost. Simple furnishings, expertly crafted, lent an inviting air to the bower. Wooden bowls and clay jars, loaded with nuts and seeds, dried fruit, and honeycomb, sat on a large table. The table legs were of white quartz. A thick slab of mica formed the top. In fact, mica was used extensively throughout the bower. Thinner strips provided excellent windows. Yellow carpet, dyed with tansy, covered the floors and offered a pleasing contrast against the dark walls.

A second door led to the bedchamber. Artemus held the door for Maeve, and the fairies eagerly crowded around. Soft light from a mica window fell upon a bed of moss, covered with a striking red velvet blanket. As Maeve turned to ask about the rare coverlet, she stumbled back in shock. There, set in a golden shell, the perfectly round reflecting glass mirrored the room, and Maeve's astonished face.

"I . . . I can't accept this," she stammered, her voice thick with emotion.

"Of course you can." Thornby said. "You lost everything. We are simply replacing what was lost."

Maeve looked at the fairies, saying nothing, and then, "Thank you," barely above a whisper. She sat on the bed, lifting a corner of the red velvet. "So soft," she murmured. "I've never seen anything like this. And the reflecting glass, where did you find these treasures?"

"Gifts from our co-worker."

"From a human?"

"That's right, by way of apology for the damage they'd caused."

This generosity was too much for Maeve. She looked away, and a hot tear slid over her cheek.

The fairies nodded and nudged one another, backing out of the doorway. Knowing that Maeve was overwhelmed, they quietly left, giving her some privacy.

"What's wrong with her?" Artemus asked Thornby. "She's not the fiery Maeve I know."

"No, she isn't."

"And not a word about where she's been all this time," Artemus said.

"I'm sure she'll tell us when she's ready. In any case, I'm glad she's back. We were all feeling worried." Thornby said.

"I hope that foolish fairy hasn't said anything," Bracken growled. Concealed in thick shrubbery, Bracken and Mugwort monitored the fairies' comings and goings, and were particularly on the lookout for human activity.

Chapter Thirty-four

Evelyn's New Friends

"Isn't that your friend Evelyn across the street?" Chris waved Beth to the window.

She walked up beside him and looked out. Evelyn stood motionless in the gathering darkness, holding up her bike, watching the house.

"What does she want?" Chris asked. "It's creepy, her just standing there like that."

Evelyn's eyes turned to the window and locked on Beth. A look of revulsion crossed her face, and the strength of it forced Beth to take a step back. Chris pulled back too.

"What did you do to her?" he asked.

"Nothing . . . Really," she added, at his disbelieving look. "She's never liked me. It's because I stand up to her."

"You're always doing that. If you were bigger, I could see it, but you're little. You're like a little dog snapping at people's ankles."

"Shut up."

"She's not here because you stand up to her. There's something wrong with that girl."

Chris was right. The look in her eyes set Beth's teeth on edge.

Evelyn swung her leg over the bike and rode off.

Detaching from the shadows, the wiggins shot across the street right up to the window, their leering mouths pressed against the glass. Beth recoiled with a sharp cry, falling to the floor.

"What happened?" Chris asked, bending over her.

Beth's face drained of color.

"Beth?" He helped her to her feet.

Evelyn and the wiggins? she thought, and looked back to the window. Two circles of slobber oozed down the glass. "I know why Evelyn is acting weird," she said.

"Why?"

"There's something I should tell you first."

"What is it?"

"Things exist that most people can't see, but I can." Chris started to cut in, and she put her hand up. "Just wait a minute. I've seen something terrible, something that was here, just outside the window." She pointed. "See that slimy stuff? That came from the wiggins."

"Wiggins."

"They're bad, very bad."

"Nothing is out there."

"You have to believe me, Chris. Evelyn and the wiggins have hooked up. Something bad is going to happen."

"I thought you were finished with that stuff."

"It's real."

"Mom and Dad don't need to know you're crazy again, so I won't tell them, but you have to pull yourself together. Why don't you just talk to Evelyn, straighten things out?"

"You think you know everything. You think you're so grown up."

"More grown up than you," Chris said. "Think about it. At least I have a social life. How many friends do you have?"

"I've been busy," Beth said, in her defense, but her heart pinched. Chris had hit a sore spot. She hadn't found one friend at school, hadn't even tried.

"Busy looking for things that aren't there. Look, Beth, you need to get a life. Go make some friends." He put his hand on her shoulder, trying to offer encouragement.

"It hurts that you don't believe me," she said quietly, and walked away.

The reproachful way Beth spoke, and the pained look in her eyes, threw Chris off. He looked at the window. Saliva slid down the pane.

Things aren't normal in this house, he thought, with a stab of

113

conscience. He knew it, or at least he sensed it. The dream he'd shared with Beth came to mind and that had been freaky. Since then, he had caught the occasional movement from the corner of his eye. Nothing he could pinpoint, but it caused his skin to crawl.

Chapter Thirty-five

An Alternate Universe

One more week of school, chimed constantly in Beth's head, as she endured another stuffy hour in class. She had successfully avoided Evelyn who sat at the back of the room, but every once in a while the hairs on her neck prickled when she sensed Evelyn looking her way.

The wiggins hadn't surfaced again, and all that Beth could hope for was that when they did Evelyn and her new friends would leave her alone.

At lunch, she sat on an empty bench and rifled through her backpack for a sandwich.

"Hi, Beth," Evelyn plunked down beside her, "mind if I sit here?"

Beth stiffened and said nothing.

"I know we don't get along very well. It's mostly my fault. I just get in a bad mood sometimes, so sorry, okay?"

Beth felt her world spinning, falling into an alternate universe. "Okay . . . sure . . . no problem," she muttered, barely above a whisper.

"We'll just start over. So, do you have any plans for the summer?"

"No," Beth said.

"I happened to ride by your place last week. The house looks better. You painted. Good color."

"Thanks."

"We used to ride over there when the place was abandoned. The yard was a pigsty."

"We cleaned it up."

"It must look way better."

"It does. I even planted some flowers."

"Really?"

The strangeness of conversing with Evelyn, as though nothing had ever happened between them, further disoriented Beth. She didn't like talking about home either, and her stomach gave a queasy lurch. "What are your plans for the summer, Evelyn?" she asked, hoping to change the subject and wishing Evelyn would leave.

"I have yard work to do too. Pruning, actually. See you around."

Beth chewed over the apology, watching Evelyn walk away. Nothing about that conversation felt right, but it would have to do. Maybe her troubles with Evelyn were over. Maybe Evelyn and the wiggins showing up together was a coincidence. It might be a good holiday after all. *One more week of school.*

Chapter Thirty-six

Summer Holidays

The last bell sounded. Funneling through the entryway, a mad crush of students burst through the doors. They cascaded down the steps, dispersing in all directions. Collective glee charged the air in that first minute of summer Vacation.

Beth peddled home filled with the possibilities of summer. She hoped to spend much of her time swimming at a nearby lake and taking time for some summer reading.

For three hours, twice a week, she had agreed to work at the bookstore, dusting, vacuuming, and doing odd jobs. What she really wanted to try was using the till and helping customers, but her parents wanted to see how she did with her other jobs first.

Wheeling into the yard, she rode her bike around to the back. A strange bicycle leaned against the porch, and her body tensed. *Is that Evelyn's bike?*

Andrew Peasgood sat at the kitchen table across from Chris. He smiled at Beth when she opened the screen door.

"Hi, Beth, how are you?"

"Good. When did you get here?"

"This morning."

Andrew looked different. His tawny hair had grown longer, curling around his neck. Blue eyes gave their full attention, and his smile caught Beth by surprise. Her pulse quickened. Spots of red painted her cheeks. She fussed with her backpack, setting it on the counter, hoping her blush would go unnoticed.

"We're riding to the falls tomorrow. Do you want to come?" Andrew's smile widened.

"Doesn't your grandmother have something planned tomorrow?" Chris asked.

"Lindsey and Alex are having a painting lesson. You're invited,

Beth, if you want to go."

She wanted to go with Andrew, but could see that Chris didn't like the idea. She hesitated.

"If you want to paint, I can take you to the falls another time," Andrew said.

"You don't want a painting lesson, Andrew?"

"No, it's not for me."

"Me neither," Chris said.

"Okay, I'll go to the falls next time." *Without Chris,* she thought. "I want to try out the swimming hole you told us about."

"You're going to love it. It's deep enough to jump off the rocks, but you won't want to stay in too long. The water is freezing."

"I was thinking that we could take a ride over to Bobby's house. He's a friend I met at school." Chris pushed away from the table. "We could hang out there for a while. Do you want to?"

"Sure." Andrew stood up and followed Chris to the door. "See you later, Beth."

She watched them ride out of the yard. *Chris doesn't know what he's talking about. I do have friends—and a social life.*

Chapter Thirty-seven

Preparations

Artemus located Thornby by the heart-racing music streaming from a patch of rhubarb.

Thornby's bow streaked across the strings, while fingers danced upon the fiddle. With eyes closed and brows furrowed, he lost himself in the music.

A foot tapped, the other itching to join in, as Artemus waited for the song to finish. Thornby continued, oblivious to his surroundings and his audience.

At length, the last note silenced.

"A compelling piece of music," Artemus said. "I could barely keep still."

Thornby started in surprise, his face flushed with excitement. "I'm composing something new for the celebration," he said, flashing a grin.

"Which is why I'm here. I've written some remarkable words, possibly my best work, and I want you to play during my presentation."

"Don't you think music would interfere with your delivery?"

"Not at all. You play first, as a prelude to my performance. Then, with my words, I will lift them to the heavens. During the stunned silence, your music can lead them back to earth. What do you say?"

"Midsummer is in five days. With so much still to be done, I'm not sure I have time to take on a new project."

"Nonsense. Vali has the preparations well in hand. Everyone has an assigned task. Come to think of it, I'm surprised you're not with the musicians right now."

"We practice this afternoon. And what about you, what is your task?"

Artemus leaned in and spoke with a solemn tone. "The Soma distiller arrives soon. My job is to see to his needs."

Thornby's eyes widened. "Soma? I thought soma distillation was a lost art. I'm amazed that a soma master could be found."

"Now that the garden is presentable, Vali warmed to the challenge. He sent out inquiries in every direction."

"I had no idea." Thornby laid the fiddle in its case.

"Recently he received news of a distiller living as a hermit in the forest. One of the council members volunteered to make the journey, and delivered a special invitation." Artemus smiled with approval. "Vali has certainly strived to recapture the splendor of the old ways, and that includes distilled light."

Thornby's heart thrilled. Four months ago, he would have settled for garbage clean-up.

Vali monitored one cluster of industrious fairies after another. They worked in small groups, spread out among the various residences. These were larger homes, built in the wild area, bordering the garden. The progress pleased him.

The master of soma had arrived to create the most celebrated, and most rare drink in the elemental realm. Soma, distilled from the very essence of light, took complete silence and the utmost privacy to create. Vali provided a comfortable house far from other dwellings to insure secrecy and quiet.

Having met the master's requirements, Artemus had been dismissed with orders not to return. He reported back to Vali, with a star-struck look in his eyes. Before Vali could give him another assignment, Artemus excused himself, stating that a poem was swirling in his head, and it needed to get out.

Vali smiled to himself. *Poets are strange beings,* he thought, watching Artemus walk away, muttering, and gesturing, no doubt turning words into treasure.

He pulled out his list and added soma to the finished column, happy that the "finished" outstripped the "to do" side.

Woven baskets bulged with nuts and seeds from last year's

cache. The scent of honey cakes filled the air. Later, the cakes would be decorated with wild strawberries. Dried apples, cherries, and wild berries sat in clay pots, soaking in honeyed syrup. All the food preparation was well underway.

Drinks, such as nectar and dew, were collected. An ancient traditional cistern, carefully preserved and used only during celebrations, brimmed with water. Made from the shell of a gourd and carved with a motif of dancers, the cistern glowed with a polished sheen. For the more robust drinkers, a cart of imported mead sat at the edge of the garden.

Tent mending fell behind schedule, and Vali walked over to the group of fairies assigned to the task, dusting off his motivational speech.

Chapter Thirty-eight

A Trip to the Falls

Stowing their bikes off the road behind some brush, Andrew and Chris entered the watershed. Canyon walls rose steeply above the trail. Giant cedars stretched to the canyon rim, their uppermost branches tipped in sunlight, with trunks plunged into shadow.

At once, Chris noticed a difference in the air. The temperature had dropped a good ten degrees. Moss covered the trees in blankets of phosphorescent green. Lichen and mushrooms grew in abundance. "It feels like we just stepped into the Lost World," he said, placing his hand on a cedar, and looking up.

The trail hugged a raging stream, swollen from the spring melt. "We'll have to cross the stream twice," Andrew said.

"How are we going to do that?"

"Over some fallen logs."

"I can hear the falls. Are we close?"

"We are, but we have some climbing to do before we get there."

The trail became an obstacle course, crawling under and climbing over a tangle of logs and debris. With every turn the roar of the water grew.

Exploding over the ledge, the falls crashed furiously onto the rocks below, thundering with the full force of spring runoff. The boys stood for a while watching its turbulent descent.

Andrew cupped his mouth, hollering into Chris's ear. "Do you want to climb above the falls?" He pointed to a steep trail.

It took some effort to reach the top, but the view was worth it. A second waterfall plummeted into a churning pool, before plunging over the ledge to form the lower falls. Mist off the water dampened their clothing, so they drew back, sitting on a large rock for a drier view.

Chris's thoughts turned to exploration. He noticed a path leading into the woods behind them. "I'd like to see where that leads," he said.

Andrew nodded, and they turned from the falls.

The trees grew smaller than the giants in the canyon below, and thick underbrush clogged the trail. A few charred stumps gave evidence of a fire long past. Here and there, a tall tree towered, lone survivors among the younger growth.

"Look at this." Andrew pointed to his arm. Three red beetles explored the contours of his shirt. "Ladybugs."

A fourth ladybug smacked against Chris's cheek. He removed the insect, holding its crisp shell gently between thumb and forefinger. Its little legs waved furiously. He placed the ladybug on his arm and watched it dawdle along a fold in his sleeve. "I wonder where these are coming from?" Its outer shell separated into flaps and tiny wings appeared, launching the ladybug onto his shoulder.

"Let's see if there's a nest nearby," Andrew suggested. A few more hitchhikers collected on their clothing.

They came across an enormous log. Its gray bark suggested years of decay. The bulk of it stretched over more fallen trees, caught like dominoes in the path of the crashing giant. Here, the ladybugs congregated in a mass of red.

"There must be hundreds of them," Chris said. Removing his passengers, he returned them to the nest. More flew out to replace them, and he watched the new invaders settle on his clothing.

"Too bad we don't have a camera," Andrew said. "I'd like to get a picture of this."

They watched the ladybugs for a while before turning away.

"Do you want to head out?" Andrew asked. "I'm starting to get hungry."

"I bet that Mom will be making lunch for everyone. If we leave now, we could get in on that."

"What if you're wrong?"

"Then I'll make lunch," Chris said.

"That ought to be good."

Chapter Thirty-nine

Painting Lesson

The group of artists assembled on the grass, their paper and paints arrayed before them. Roses, the subject of their lesson, reflected the morning sun.

"I'd like you to lightly draw the roses," Mrs. Peasgood said. "Don't worry if the drawing isn't perfect."

Even though Mrs. Peasgood said not to worry, Beth did. She wanted the roses to look right.

"The drawing is just a guideline," Mrs. Peasgood said, noticing Beth's furrow of concentration. "We'll paint over the pencil lines anyway." She waited for her students to complete their drawings.

"Are you ready to paint? Let's give it a try. Using clean water, I'd like you to paint one rose petal."

"You mean without paint?" Lindsey asked.

"Like this." With a clean brush, Mrs. Peasgood lifted clear water onto the paper, filling in just one petal. Then she slipped her brush into the red, dropping the color onto the wet. The red fanned out, at once soft as a petal and brilliant with color.

"One more thing before you start. The sun is on our left, and you can see a bit of reflection on the roses." She pulled a tissue from her pocket and dabbed a corner of the still wet petal, lifting some color.

"That makes it look like sunshine on the flower," Alex said, already applying red to his painting.

By late morning, everyone's paintings were shaping up nicely. Beth's mother arrived with a tray of lemonade. "All of you are doing so well," she said, examining their handiwork. She put the tray down on the grass and sat beside it, pouring a glass for everyone, including herself. "The pruning certainly brought out the best in those roses," she said.

"They're surprisingly hardy plants, and they spring back quite well with the right attention," Mrs. Peasgood said. "Good job, Beth."

"When you've finished your paintings," Beth's mother rose to her feet, "come up to the house for lunch. Then we'll have an art exhibition. I'm afraid we don't have time to send out invitations or write a press release," she grinned.

"That's okay, Mom, we'll have a private showing."

"I can't let the day go by without smelling the roses." Beth's mom bent over the nearest rose bush and buried her nose into the velvet petals. "What a wonderful smell. Often, the roses these days don't have much of a scent." She wandered around the bushes, admiring the blooms. On the far side she paused, frowning. "What's happening here?" she asked, stooping to examine leaves loaded with insects.

Everyone walked over to see what she had found. Thousands of small green bugs collected along the ribs of each leaf, sucking up the sap. Many leaves had withered, crisping and browning at the edges.

Chris and Andrew pulled into the yard, and noticing the group clustered around the rose bushes, walked over to join them. "What are you looking at?" Andrew asked.

"Aphids." Mrs. Peasgood said.

Beth folded her arms, frowning. "How can I get rid of them?" she asked, worried that the answer might involve bug spray.

"You can spray the aphids with water, but you'll have to take care not to soak the flowers." Mrs. Peasgood said. "Just blast the leaves using lots of water pressure to knock them off. You can repeat the process in four or five days, to be sure you got them all."

"They look like tiny pouches of green syrup," Andrew said, leaning closer to examine the aphids.

"What do we have here?" Mrs. Peasgood lifted a ladybug crawling out from under Andrew's collar. She set the beetle onto a leaf, and everyone moved forward to see what would happen. The ladybug lit into an aphid, polishing it off in no time, then grabbed another. "Aphids are a ladybug's favorite food."

"Why not use ladybugs instead of water? We found a whole

bunch of them," Andrew suggested.

"What would you like to do, Beth?" her mother asked.

"I'd like to get some more ladybugs. Could we go after lunch?"

"I don't feel like going back there again today," Chris said.

"So don't." Beth turned to Andrew. "Do you feel like going?"

"I guess so," Andrew said.

"I want to go," Alex said, inviting himself along.

"I'll go," Lindsey said.

"Sure, why not. I might as well go too," Chris said, casting a sidelong glance at Lindsey.

"I'm glad you're going," his mother said, "You can look out for Beth and Alex."

Beth didn't like being grouped with Alex. She was almost twelve, not a baby. She lifted her chin. "I can look after myself, don't worry."

"Then it's settled," Mrs. Peasgood said, "ladybugs it is."

Chapter Forty

Hitchhikers

This can't be happening. Bracken watched in disbelief as the humans grouped around the roses, examining the aphids. He motioned his team in closer. "Lichen, Vetch," he said in a low voice, "You stay here. Keep an eye out for intruders."

"Why? Who's coming?" Vetch asked.

"Shhhh, keep it down. Be on the look out for fairies. If they spot us, the game is over." Bracken gritted his teeth in exasperation. Why did he have to bring that empty-headed toad along? King's cousin or not, Vetch could easily compromise the campaign. "Lichen," he spoke with a sarcastic edge, "keep an eye on Vetch. Don't let him wander off." Bracken placed a hand on Mugwort's shoulder. "Mugwort, you're with me."

They crawled on their bellies, inching close enough to listen in. Bracken almost laughed when one of the humans set a ladybug on top of an aphid. "One ladybug won't be a problem," he whispered to Mugwort. "I don't think we have anything to worry about."

"We found a whole bunch," a boy informed the group.

"Now that could be a problem," Mugwort said.

They listened carefully, and when the humans left for the house, Bracken rallied his team. "We have a mission. We're going to take a little trip."

"What's the mission?" Lichen asked.

"What we do best, sabotage."

They rode in a single file, Chris taking the lead. The imps sat on the front fenders of the first four bikes, their faces to the wind, red hair streaming, confident in their invisibility.

Chris slowed his bike and let Lindsey pass, hanging back to talk to Beth. "Seen any wiggins lately?"

"No." Beth hissed under her breath. "I don't want to talk about it."

"What about poltergeists or trolls, seen any of those?"

"Shut up." She glanced back to see if Andrew was listening. He and Alex had fallen back and were carrying on a conversation of their own. The relief she felt surprised her, and she realized that she liked Andrew. It was bad enough that Chris thought she was crazy. It would be awful if Andrew thought so too.

Actually, she had been seeing things—red blurry blotches—on and off all day. It was getting annoying. She didn't know what to make of them and hoped they would go away.

A car sped along the road forcing Chris to pull in ahead. Beth settled into her thoughts and peddled in silence.

Bracken enjoyed this mode of transportation. He sat back on Beth's fender taking in the sights and thinking about the conversation he'd just heard. *Trolls, we could give them trolls.* A brilliant idea took shape.

Arriving at the entrance to the falls, they pulled their bikes off the road. Everyone carried a canvas bag to transport the ladybugs. The porous weave would let in enough air until they could get the beetles home.

The mid-afternoon sun lowered toward the canyon wall. Long shafts of light pierced through the trees, releasing a fragrance of cedar.

"I hope we didn't leave this too late," Beth said, eyeing the deepening shadows.

"There's plenty of time," Andrew said, stepping up to walk beside her.

With the lowering sun, the temperature in the canyon had dropped dramatically. *I wish I'd brought a sweater,* Beth thought, chafing the goose bumps on her arms.

Bracken and his team ran ahead, looking for the best spot for an ambush. They stationed themselves where the trail rose up, hugging the canyon wall.

"Most of this area is shale," Bracken said, pointing to a jutting shelf above. "We'll climb up and loosen some." The imps worked swiftly. Each gathered a pile of rocks to push and waited for Bracken's signal.

Chris led them up the path, just as the imps heaved their rocks over the shelf, raining on the people below. Chris and Lindsey threw themselves against the wall where an outcropping protected them from the worst of it. The others cried out and flinging their arms over their heads, pelted back down the path.

The hail of stones stopped.

"Everyone all right?" Chris asked.

Lindsey held her forehead. "Okay," she said, but her eyes welled with tears.

"We're all right," Beth shouted.

Chris examined Lindsey's forehead. "What do you want to do? Do you want to go home?"

"No, I'm fine."

"Are you sure? It looks like an egg is forming."

"Positive."

"That's never happened before," Andrew said, climbing back up the path with Beth and Alex. He looked up, studying the rock shelf. I could see maybe one stone falling, but not an avalanche.

"I think we should get down from here," Alex said.

They followed the trail back down to the canyon floor and continued on toward the falls. The imps watched from their perch.

"They're a plucky bunch, I'll give them that," Bracken said, grudgingly. "Let's go, boys, we'll need to get ahead of them." He shot down the path to take the lead. "Keep up. I have an idea."

The falls cascaded into a pool studded with rocks. Bracken paced up and down the bank, studying the area. He noted that where the stream widened a group of stones formed a natural bridge to the opposite side. The water looked shallow there, but boiled with whirlpools and eddies. Then he noticed the cave, and his plan took shape.

He beckoned to his waiting crew and pointed. "There's a cave behind the falls, and we'll use it to make a sending."

"Of what?" Vetch grumbled.

"Of a water troll."

"There's no such thing."

Bracken rolled his eyes skyward. "It doesn't matter. The sending isn't real anyway."

"I'm no good at sendings," Vetch said, grating on Bracken's last nerve.

"You'll do it and you'll do it well. Anyone else have a problem?" He drew himself up, hands balled into fists.

"No, no problem," they all muttered.

"Let's get on with it. They'll be coming soon." Bracken ushered his team to the water's edge. "Put the troll in the cave. Be sure they can see his ugly face through the water. I want them scared and running out of here."

"Last summer, we climbed in there," Andrew said to Beth, pointing to the cave. They all gathered by the water's edge to watch the falls. "Later, in the summer when there's less water, we'll come back and you can try it."

"Is it a big cave?"

"Not really. There's enough room for four or five people, but it's fun to stand in there and look out through the water."

"Doesn't it look like a big face in there?"

"It does. I never noticed that before."

By some unspoken signal, they all turned at once and headed for the rock stepping stones. Crossing easily, they climbed onto the opposite bank. From there, the path continued, leading up a steep slope, ending at the upper falls.

"Fools," Bracken shouted. "It was a simple sending!"

Heads hanging, the team stammered their excuses. "Out of practice." "Not enough time."

"No matter, let them get their ladybugs. We'll catch them on the way back." The imps nodded vigorously. It was rare to receive a second chance from Bracken.

He hopped onto a rock and looked down on his team. "This time we'll lay the troll in the water, right where they have to cross. Make it look bad. I want big teeth and nasty claws," he said, slamming fist into hand. "Don't overlook the eyes. That was shoddy work last time."

Vetch was tempted to remind Bracken that he also contributed to that last sending, but good sense prevailed.

"Make the eyes red," Bracken continued, "and more predatory. Are we clear? Good, start concentrating, lads. This time we'll be ready."

Chapter Forty-one

Sabotage

They clambered up the steep path with hands and feet, topping the rim. Here the sun shone fully, leaving the canyon in shadow. It took a few moments to catch their breath.

"Check this out." Andrew pointed to a deep cleft.

Carved by countless years of rushing water, a maelstrom of foam plunged to a pool below. Sunlight cast rainbows in the plumes of spray.

"This is my favorite place," Lindsey said. "It's so wild." Strands of damp hair clung to her face. She closed her eyes, spreading her arms, and allowed the mist to overtake her.

Watching Lindsey, Beth imagined an ancient warrior woman, hair flowing, absorbing the wildness of the water. She stepped up beside Lindsey and breathed deeply, instantly feeling energized. Though it could have come from the freshness of air and mist, Beth preferred to think that the falls had bestowed the gift of strength. She laughed into the roar of rushing water. Lindsey grinned, seeming to guess her thoughts.

"What about the ladybugs?" Alex asked, reminding them of their quest.

"I guess we should go," Andrew said, taking a last look at the falls. "The nest is over there."

Following the crest of the canyon, they came across the massive log. A few ladybugs stood out, red against gray.

"This log was crawling with ladybugs earlier," Chris said, watching the dawdling beetles.

"I bet we'll find more if we peel back some of the bark," Andrew said, when a ladybug burrowed beneath a thick slab.

Chris pulled off a chunk of bark, revealing a cache of bugs. "Not too many left, maybe a hundred, give or take," he said.

"Where did they go?" Alex asked.

"I think they hatched here and moved on when the food supply was used up," Andrew said. "By tomorrow, these ladybugs will probably be gone too."

"It looks like we'll only need one bag," Beth said, spreading the opening and carefully placing some beetles inside. The others joined in the ladybug roundup, until all the bugs were safely stowed.

"This should be enough to do the job." Beth slung the bag over her shoulder, and they returned to the rim of the canyon.

It looks much steeper going down, Beth thought, looking over the edge. Without hesitation, Alex dropped onto the path, and the others followed, making their descent.

Carefully, Beth eased herself over, sliding several feet on her bottom. With a stab of panic, she dug her heels into the dirt and stopped. Waiting a moment to collect herself, she watched the others, noting that no one slid on the seat of their pants. She stood and half sliding, half hopping, managed a few more feet, before grabbing a branch to slow herself and sitting to stop.

Below, Lindsey moved confidently, and Beth watched with admiration. She thought of the strength she had felt when standing by the falls and tried to summon that feeling. *Come on, you can do this.* Taking a breath and letting it out, she willed herself to relax. Looking around her, she took in the fullness of the trees and the openness of the sky. A sense of strength filled her, not solid and weighty, but light, as a gift bestowed by the air. A thought moved in quickly to insist that it was her imagination, but she squashed it. Her body, of its own will, rose, and before thought could intervene, she leapt.

This feels like flying! Stopping came easily when she used her heels. Spreading her arms, she launched off again, continuing down the path with mountain goat surety.

Everyone looked up, watching her technique with amazement.

"I have to try that next time," Alex said. "It looks like fun."

Ranged on the opposite side of the stream, the imps gathered for their final instructions.

"Timing is everything," Bracken said. "Do not form the troll until the group has climbed onto the rocks and is crossing the stream."

They stood along the bank, the elite team of four—the king's eyes and ears—each preparing mentally for the task. All felt confident that they would succeed.

Lindsey saw it first, a hideous apparition below the water. "What is that?" she shrieked, pointing with disbelief.

Everyone looked. Unable to process what they were seeing, they stood frozen in fascinated horror. Red eyes bored into them. The long gash, which served as the creature's mouth, opened wide, ringed with razor teeth. Still no one moved, shock cementing them to the spot.

The mouth trembled, and its jaws unhinged, expanding to cavernous black.

"Get out of here now," Chris shouted, tearing his eyes away.

Roused by the shout, panic took hold, and they bolted across the rocks.

Beth lost her footing and toppled into the open maw. Icy water closed over her, its turbulence pinning her under. Any second, the mouth would clamp shut and she would be lost.

Kicking her feet, her toes met with gravel—or maybe a rough tongue. She pushed off in terror, propelling to the surface, and sucking in air. The churning water pulled her down, and although it wasn't deep, the current made it difficult to get her footing again. Her body spun along the gravel and slammed into a rock. What little air remained blew out with the impact.

Chris jumped. Though waist deep, the pull of the water threatened to sweep him under. He could see Beth directly through the creature, which had stretched to a thin transparency. Anchoring his foot against the rock, he reached, grabbing onto her shirt, and then he dragged her thrashing body to the surface.

She rocketed from the water gasping and choking.

"It's all right, Beth, I have you."

"Where is it?" she sputtered, wildly searching the water.

"It's gone."

"Beth, give me your hand," Andrew shouted, and pulled her onto the bank. Chris sprawled beside her, their bodies shaking with cold.

"I want to go home," Beth said, and dissolved into tears.

"I'm so sorry, Beth." Chris said, through chattering teeth.

"What for?"

"Because I've been seeing things too. Not like you have, just weird shadows sometimes."

The look of hurt on Beth's face said it all, and he burned with shame. "I didn't want people to think I was losing it, so I pretended nothing was there. But after today . . . I'm really sorry."

"We have to go," Lindsey said.

"Beth?"

"It's okay, Chris, forget about it." Wiping her eyes with the heels of her hands she got to her feet. "So much for the ladybugs," she said, frowning at the soggy bag.

Chris's eyes widened. As one, the others followed his gaze, shocked by what they saw. Four small figures gathered on the path. Unaware that they had an audience, they clapped each other on the back and shook hands, congratulating themselves. They stood about a foot tall, with shocks of bright red hair. One of them pointed at the water and doubled over with laughter. When he straightened, the laughter died.

"Are they looking at us? Can they see us?" Vetch asked, backing away.

"Don't be a fool," Bracken snapped, "That's not p . . ." The smallest human pointed straight at him. "Run!" Bracken ran for cover diving into a tangle of bushes.

How could this happen? Bracken wondered, as his team gathered beside him.

"This is your fault," Vetch said. The others clearly agreed.

The sending, of course. Bracken smacked his forehead. It had been so long since anyone had attempted a sending, and he had forgotten about the side effects. *Everyone knows the connection between the senders and those receiving the sending always strengthened. How could something that important slip my mind?* Now the imps were plainly visible. "What's done is done," he said.

"We'll wait until they leave and follow them back."

"You mean walk?" Mugwort asked, scowling in protest.

"We can't exactly ask them for a lift, now can we."

"Let's get out of here," Andrew said.

"What are those things?" Alex asked.

"I don't know, but we're not sticking around to find out."

They left the canyon as quickly as they could and rode home. By the time they pulled into the yard, Beth's and Chris's teeth clicked together in drum rolls and their bodies shook.

Beth pried her icy fingers from the handlebars. "I'm going in for a hot bath."

"Me too," Chris said.

"We should get together later," Lindsey said, "and talk about what happened."

Chapter Forty-two

Red-Haired Short People

Mrs. Peasgood stood at the counter preparing dinner. The door opened and she turned to greet her grandchildren, but her words froze. Lindsey, her forehead purpled by a large welt, flung herself on to the nearest chair.

"We've had some trouble," Andrew said.

"So I see. Are you boys all right? What about Chris and Beth?" Mrs. Peasgood asked, leaning over Lindsey to examine her forehead.

"We're all okay," Alex said.

"I want to hear what happened, but first let me look at your forehead, Lindsey. Do you have a headache?" Mrs. Peasgood probed the injury with gentle fingers.

"No."

"Dizzy?"

"No."

"Good. What about sleepy?"

"I'm tired, but I don't feel like sleeping."

"All right, I'll make a poultice to help bring down the swelling. Andrew, Alex, please sit down and tell me what happened."

"Something didn't want us to get the ladybugs," Andrew said.

"Something?"

"I'm not sure what they are." Andrew shook his head and looked to the others to help explain.

"They were little guys," Alex said, "with red hair that stuck out like horse tails."

"Red-haired, short people?" Mrs. Peasgood eyed her grandchildren with a puzzled look.

"No, really short." Alex held his hand about a foot off the table. Andrew and Lindsey nodded.

Andrew told his grandmother about the rockslide, the monster in the water, Beth falling in, and then the little people laughing by the water's edge.

"They're small," Alex said, "but I think they're dangerous. They look like little soldiers."

The phone rang, and Mrs. Peasgood rose to answer it. She listened for a moment. "That's probably best," she said. "Why don't you and Chris come by in the morning for breakfast? How about nine o'clock? All right, see you then, goodbye."

"Chris's and Beth's parents are unhappy with them right now. We won't see them until tomorrow." She said, hanging up the phone. "Now, about those little people." Mrs. Peasgood seated herself, but said nothing. Her grandchildren looked at one another and waited.

Andrew broke the silence. "What do you think, Grams?" It was a measure of the trust between Mrs. Peasgood and her grandchildren that little, red-haired people were not dismissed as impossible. "Do you think they might be fairies?"

"Fairies? No, they're not fairies, but certainly from the elemental realm."

"What's the elemental realm?" Lindsey asked.

"It's the fairy realm. They're nature spirits of some kind, connected to the elements of earth, air, fire, and water. For example, dwarves are of the earth, living underground. Many stories depict them as miners and metalsmiths."

"It's great that you believe in this stuff," Andrew said. "A lot of people wouldn't."

"And I'd be one of those people, had I not experienced some extraordinary occurrences over the years. There's something special about this place."

"So you've seen those little creatures?" Lindsey asked.

"No, nothing like that. But, I don't doubt that you have."

"I've always hoped there'd be cute little fairies," Lindsey said.

"Bunnies are cute. Dealings with the elementals must always be cautious and respectful. Just like the world we live in, you'll find good and bad, and all the ranges in between."

"These red-haired things are definitely bad," Andrew said. "I want to know what they are and what they want with us."

"The names sprites, gremlins, and imps come to mind," Mrs. Peasgood said. "I have a few books that might help us identify these beings."

"What's going on up there?" Mugwort called to Bracken.

"Quiet. It's hard enough to hear over this wind." Bracken clung to the topmost branch of a shrub, directly in front of the kitchen window. The first drops of rain fell heavily on his head, and he tightened his grip in the increasing wind.

Inside, the children recounted their story. Bracken smiled at the description of the rockslide. *Yes, that went well. They certainly tell a good tale,* he thought, relishing the part about the troll. *True, it was a mistake, but how gratifying to watch that girl tumble into the mouth of a waiting troll. That was pure artistry.*

"What are they saying?" Mugwort shouted.

"Just wait."

The raindrops thickened, and Mugwort settled into a clump of lemon balm for shelter. The plant offered little comfort, and his thoughts turned to a warm meal and a dry bed.

Even with the imp's acute sense of hearing, Bracken found himself straining to hear against the wind.

"Sprites, gremlins, and imps," the woman said.

Incredulous, he leaned in to catch every word. The wind whipped around from behind and his nose flattened against the glass with a painful thwack. Losing his grip, he fell with a curse onto the imp below.

"What's the matter with you?" Mugwort cried from the wreckage.

"No time for that, we've got trouble." Bracken pulled Mugwort to his feet, and signaling the other imps, they rushed back to camp.

Mrs. Peasgood returned to the dinner preparations, while

her grandchildren went upstairs for hot showers and a change of clothes. Sliding a casserole into the oven, she adjusted the temperature. She then reached for some scissors and stepped outside. Rain fell, and the wind blew. She hurried to the garden.

A sizeable herb garden stretched along the side of the house. Among the culinary herbs, such as basil and dill, Mrs. Peasgood had planted an array of medicinal plants. Not only were they useful for a variety of ailments, but also their delicate flowers and leafy foliage lent an unrestrained look to an otherwise orderly garden.

She cut some leaves and dug a piece of root from a comfrey plant, rinsing them under the garden hose. The gusting wind carried the water sideways in a spray. Looking up she saw massive dark clouds promising heavier rain.

Back at the kitchen counter she chopped the leaves and root, placing them in a pot to simmer. Before long, the comfrey produced a gelatinous, slimy goo.

"Just right," She scooped the hot mixture onto a cloth and folded the compress, setting it aside to cool.

By the time her grandchildren returned to the table, they were ravenous. Mrs. Peasgood taped the compress onto Lindsey's forehead, and they all sat down to dinner. Too hungry and tired to speak, they dug in with grateful silence.

Chapter Forty-three

Elemental

They're on the move." Bracken alerted the imps from his tree perch. They concealed themselves in the leafy foliage below.

A short time later, Beth and Chris passed directly under the tree, unaware of the watchers.

From the direction they were headed, Bracken was certain they'd be joining the other children, and that worried him. However, more worrisome was this woman who spoke of imps.

"Follow them," he ordered. The waiting group burst from behind the tree and leapt onto the path, trotting behind the children. "No, fall back," Bracken hissed, dropping to the ground. "They'll see you." The imps dove for cover in a thick patch of periwinkle, lying flat on their bellies.

As if on cue, Beth and Chris paused, looking back.

"I thought I heard something," Beth said.

"Me too; I get the feeling we're not alone. Let's check it out. Maybe we'll find our little friends."

Beth's brow creased in concern. "Let's just go. I don't want to find them. They're creepy."

Chris retraced his steps and spoke over his shoulder. "Don't worry. They're little. They should be afraid of us."

"They're coming back," Bracken whispered, melting farther into the ground cover. The four imps lay still, hardly breathing, as the boy approached. Bracken, who prided himself as an expert tracker, was appalled. He now understood how much difficulty their visibility could cause.

"There." The boy pointed. To his horror, Bracken saw Vetch's hair resting on top of the foliage.

As irresistible as a dog after a stick, Chris burst upon the imps, shouting and waving his arms. Flushed from their cover, the imps bolted like red rabbits.

Chris laughed. "That's right, run."

Beth did not share his enthusiasm. "Why did you do that? It's like throwing a rock at a wasp nest."

"It's not the same thing at all, and it felt great."

A half-moon of milk glossed Beth's lip, and she wiped it with her sleeve. Eyeing the remaining waffles, she wondered if she had room for a third.

Chris had no such doubts and stabbed another, setting it on his plate. The waffle transformed to an island, surrounded by thick maple syrup.

"These are great waffles, Mrs. Peasgood." He polished off the third with as much relish as the first.

Mrs. Peasgood poured the last bit of tea into their cups. "Shall I heat more water? Does anyone want more tea?" Everyone felt that they'd had enough, so she set the teapot back on the table. "Now that we've finished breakfast, it's time to get down to business. Let's talk about what happened yesterday. Was this your first encounter with the red-haired beings?"

"Yes," Chris said, "but we saw them again this morning on the way over here. I think they were following us."

Everyone turned to the window to see if they were being spied upon, but they were quite alone.

"Chris chased them away," Beth said. "They're gone for now."

"And they scattered like rabbits," Chris said with a satisfied smirk.

"Was that a good idea, Chris?" Mrs. Peasgood said. "We don't know what they are yet, but they've demonstrated that they can be dangerous. I think we need to be cautious."

"I do too," Beth said.

"It's rare to see any beings from the fairy realm. I'm surprised that they've revealed themselves," Mrs. Peasgood said.

"I've spoken to a fairy."

Everyone turned to Beth in surprise.

"When was that?" Mrs. Peasgood asked.

Beth smiled at Mrs. Peasgood's easy acceptance. There was never an "Are you sure?" or "What an active imagination." Mrs. Peasgood always listened with interest, and Beth knew that this time would be no exception.

"It was after the garden party when I first met Thornby. That's the fairy's name. He said that all the fairies were upset when we towed the truck away. Next time he wants us to let the fairies know what we're doing in the garden. We talked again just before I fertilized the flowerbeds."

Everyone started asking questions at once. "What did he look like?" "How tall was he?"

"This big." Beth indicated four or five inches with her thumb and forefinger.

Chris frowned. "You didn't tell me about this. Why not?"

"It saved a lot of trouble by keeping it secret." She gave him a pointed look.

"I said I was sorry. It's hard to believe when you see things and I don't." His eyes widened. "Hey, are you going to tell them about the wiggins?"

"What's a wiggin?" Alex asked.

Beth described the wiggins and told about her encounters, leaving out that her parents thought she might be crazy. "Thornby told me that they have no real power and needed fear or anger to become strong. If you ignore them, they go away."

"When did you last see one?" Mrs. Peasgood asked.

"A few weeks ago."

"Good. Hopefully they're gone. For now, let's concentrate on the problem at hand." She rose from the table, returning with a thick book, entitled *The World of Faerie*. The book contained marvelous drawings of both beautiful and hideous creatures.

"These are simply an artist's renderings," Mrs. Peasgood explained, "not likely accurate depictions." She thumbed through the book. "However, the text provides interesting lore describing the elemental realm. Every country has its own beliefs concerning fairies and other creatures as well."

Everyone crowded around Mrs. Peasgood to get a better look at the pictures as she turned the pages.

"I read a bit last night," she said, "and marked some possibilities."

"What did you come up with?" Chris asked.

"Boggarts, imps, goblins, and gremlins. But it really doesn't matter what we call them. What matters is what to do about them."

"I want to give them a name. We can't keep calling them red-haired things," Alex said. "Let's call them boggarts. I like how that sounds. BOWGAARTSS."

"Boggarts will be fine." Mrs. Peasgood gave Alex a broad smile.

"You said you've had some extraordinary experiences, Grams," Lindsey said. "Will you tell us about them?"

"Mostly just sensing harmony and then, later, sadness from the garden, but on several occasions, I've encountered a fairy."

"Grams, why didn't you tell us?" Lindsey asked.

"Special events in one's life are like little jewels in the heart. To speak of them, one must choose the right time and the right people. You are the right people, and I think this is the right time." She closed the book, and everyone returned to their chairs.

"One very hot summer, I was playing in the woods with my sister, Barbara. The afternoon sweltered, and we found a mossy area in the shade to sit. That's when we saw her. At first glance, in the shadows, we thought it was a dragonfly. But on closer inspection, we saw that it was a fairy. She slept soundly on the moss and didn't hear us. We watched for a while and then tiptoed away so as not to disturb her."

"What did she look like, Grams?" Andrew asked.

"Very small, only a few inches. She wore a filmy dress, almost the color of the moss."

"Camouflage." Alex piped in.

"That's right. She blended very well with her surroundings. I especially remember her face, delicate and out of keeping with her hair, which lay thick and wild about her shoulders."

"Did she have pointed ears?" Beth asked. "Thornby does."

"I don't remember, but she had transparent wings, which is why we first mistook her for a dragonfly."

"Thornby didn't have wings."

"My understanding is there are different kinds of fairies. Also, there's a wide range of beings, from the tiniest fairies to creatures of human size, perhaps bigger."

The gruesome thing in the water came to everyone's mind. Their thoughts turned uneasily to all the possible creatures out there, just lying in wait.

"Speaking of fairies, Beth, could you talk to Thornby and ask him what is going on?" Mrs. Peasgood asked.

"I can try, but I'm not sure I can reach him. Each time we met it was unexpected."

"But first, will you tell us about the other fairy, Grams?" Lindsey pressed.

"Yes, but to do that, we'll go to the painting studio. I have something to show you. Leave everything on the table. We'll take care of it later."

Chapter Forty-four

Eavesdropping

The night's rainstorm had passed, and the morning began with sunshine. Bracken found it easier to eavesdrop on the human's conversation without the noise of the rain and wind. He clung to the window frame and listened. Beside him, Vetch shifted for a better grip.

"This is humiliating," Vetch whined.

"Next time you'll make sure that red thatch of yours stays below the leaves." Bracken snapped. "It's the only solution I could come up with, so quit complaining."

In his heart, Bracken cringed with embarrassment. If any other imps caught him in this ridiculous headgear, the jokes would never end.

After the incident with the boy, Bracken ordered the imps to weave hairnets, which effectively pinned their glorious hair flat against their skulls, rendering them less visible. The necessity of this disguise infuriated Bracken but he would never let his companions know. And to be honest, he knew this visibility fiasco rested firmly on his shoulders.

Inside, all the humans sat at a table, eating their morning meal. Finally, their conversation came around to the imps. The boy who had chased them sat with his back to the window, but Bracken could hear his words clearly.

"We saw them again this morning on the way over here. I think they were following us."

Everyone turned to the window, and Bracken and Vetch had just enough time to hang below the windowsill.

"And they scattered like rabbits."

Bracken caught the words when he hoisted himself up for another look. "Rabbits indeed. You'll find out just how frightening an imp can be," he muttered. The woman advised against chasing the creatures, citing that they could be dangerous. "You bet we are." Bracken's brow pulled into a fierce scowl.

Wiggins were mentioned, something Bracken knew nothing about nor did the subject hold any interest. His attention drifted, imagining what he would do to get even with the boy.

The old tricks, such as souring milk, didn't work anymore. Few people even had cows. No, it would have to be something better than that.

Bracken's attention returned to the conversation inside. "We're about to be named," he whispered to Vetch, after the woman listed what she thought might be possibilities. *You have to hand it to those humans,* he thought, *they can be clever.*

"Boggarts?" Bracken sputtered, nearly losing his grip. "Those pasty-faced, pointy-nosed slackers?" he amended his thoughts on human cleverness.

It was decided that one of the children would talk to a fairy.

"What fairy? Vetch, did you catch the name?"

"Thorny, I think."

This could jeopardize the whole mission, Bracken thought. *Where are they going?* To his dismay, the humans left the room.

Bracken and Vetch dropped to the ground joining Mugwort and Lichen, who had been keeping watch for possible intruders.

"We have to get inside," Bracken said.

"We can't. The window is covered with some kind of mesh, and the door is closed. There's no way in," Vetch folded his arms and lifted his chin with defiance.

"This is why I'm in charge. There's not a drop of imagination among you." Bracken looked at each of them in turn. "Think once in a while, and take some initiative. Now follow me to the door."

"There are two doors," Lichen said, looking up at the imposing barriers.

"That will work to our advantage," Bracken said. The first door was screened and opened easily. "Mugwort and Vetch, hold the first door open while Lichen helps me up."

Lichen boosted Bracken up the screen door.

He stepped onto Lichen's shoulders. Stretching his fingers over a horizontal piece of wood, he pulled himself up. Now he was level with the inside doorknob.

"Will you be able to turn it?" Lichen asked.

"Of course. We're imps. We're strong. Now I want you to bring me in close to the inner door."

Expecting them to ease him in slowly, he was ill-prepared when they simply let go. The door crashed into place, mashing Bracken into the knob. The slamming door would most certainly have alerted the humans, had it not been for Bracken's body absorbing the noise.

Biting back an angry growl, he tackled the doorknob. The metal orb was indeed difficult to turn, and he pushed with all his strength. *I can't let them see me fail.* With a satisfying click, the door swung open.

The imps crowded on the doorstep, ready to bolt at the first sign of humans. The room was empty. Hearing voices from deeper in the house, they confidently entered the kitchen.

Before Bracken could stop them, Vetch and Mugwort broke from the group, charging toward the table, scrambling up a chair, and disappearing over the tabletop.

"Get down from there," Bracken demanded. He heard smacking sounds and muffled exclamations of delight. Two heads appeared over the table edge.

"You have to try this," Vetch insisted.

Mugwort nodded in agreement, cheeks too expanded for speech.

"There's no time for that." Bracken motioned for them to come down.

"We're taking initiative." Vetch smirked and motioned for Bracken and Lichen to join them.

Bracken knew there was no chance of persuading Vetch. Being the king's cousin, Vetch was spoiled and stubborn. "Very well," Bracken conceded, "but only for a moment. We have a job to do." He hoisted himself over the table edge, Lichen right behind. "What's so important that we have to waste valuable time?" he asked, striding across the table, until he faced Vetch and Mugwort. "And look at our position. We're right in the line of sight should any humans return."

Cradled in Vetch's arms lay a sizeable piece of bread. Its curious pattern of squares glistened with pockets of dark syrup.

"Bracken, you have to try this," Vetch coaxed, sweeping a handful of syrup into his mouth. Closing his eyes, Vetch rolled the syrup over his tongue, following with several loud smacks. "Sweet and delicious," he said. "We must take some for the king and queen. This food is fit for royalty."

Bracken sampled the fare, and his stern face collapsed in surprise. "Yes, we will bring some back to camp," he agreed. Elbowing his way through Vetch and Mugwort, he tore another piece of bread, dipping it in syrup.

"Give it a try, Lichen, There's plenty to go around." Mugwort waved him over.

"Here's what we are going to do," Bracken said. "Vetch, you and Mugwort stay here. See if you can find a container to transport the syrup. If you are able to carry some bread, do so, but the syrup is most important. Lichen, you're with me."

At the edge of the table, Bracken paused and turned around. "Be alert. At the first sign of trouble, head for the door."

Chapter Forty-five

Something Unusual

An artist's studio holds fascination for most visitors, and Mrs. Peasgood's studio was no exception. Stacks of paintings and sketches claimed the floor, chairs, and tables, while others were prominently displayed.

The children wandered around the room admiring the work. They commented on the different art materials crowding one of the tables and asked questions about a work in progress. This was a large canvas, propped on an easel.

"I'm using acrylics on this painting." Mrs. Peasgood replied to one of their questions. "What you see here is an under painting. I'll apply more paint, building color in layers."

"What does the art studio have to do with the other fairy?" Chris asked.

"It has everything to do with this painting over here," Mrs. Peasgood said, pointing.

Chris moved in closer. "I've seen this before," he said, lightly running his fingers over the texture of the painting. "No, I've dreamed this before." He turned to Mrs. Peasgood, eyebrows raised in question.

"With so many wonderful subjects to paint, I was a frequent visitor to the garden. But this painting is more special than the rest." She looked at everyone in turn. "Do you see anything unusual about it?"

They all crowded around the painting, examining every inch. All agreed that it was a very good painting, but no one saw anything unusual.

"For this composition, I set my easel up by the birches. I remember congratulating myself on catching the light at just the right time. The sun had lowered, casting long shadows and deepening the surrounding color." She pointed to the painting.

"These forget-me-nots especially attracted me."

"They look like blue stars in the grass," Lindsey said.

"I thought that too." Mrs. Peasgood smiled at her granddaughter. "The work went well. When I finished painting the trees, I focused on the grass and forget-me-nots. That's when I discovered the fairy watching me. I nodded in greeting, but chose not to speak, thinking I might scare her off. She seemed surprised that I could see her but didn't leave. I continued working, becoming absorbed in the act of applying paint to canvas. When next I looked, the fairy had moved from the grass and now stood right beside me, watching me paint."

"What did you do, Grams? Didn't you want to talk to her?" Andrew asked.

"In a sense, I felt like we were communicating. My mind took on a dreamy quality. Brushing fell into a rhythm, and the painting unfolded effortlessly. I felt no need for thought or fuss, and lost all track of time. By the last brushstroke, the fairy was gone."

Mrs. Peasgood stepped back a few paces and moved her arm in an expansive gesture. "Compare this painting with the others," she said, indicating a wall with pictures of all shapes and sizes. "I'm happy with my work, but this one in particular glows. It's full of light and color, and is the best painting I have ever done."

I think it's your best painting too," Lindsey said.

"But I can't take all the credit. It was a collaborative work."

"You think the fairy helped you paint this?" Beth asked.

"I do, but there's a little more to this story. When I stepped back to view the painting, I spotted the fairy standing in the grass—just a flash from the corner of my eye."

"By the trees again?" Lindsey asked.

"No, in the painting."

"I never saw the fairy. Where is she?" Chris asked.

"That's the odd thing. Not everyone notices."

"Why didn't you mention the fairy the first time I saw the painting?" Beth asked.

"If you didn't see the fairy, there was no point in bringing it up."

Everyone moved closer for a better look and then moved back, studying the picture from different angles.

"I don't see anything," Beth said, looking disappointed. She thought because of her meetings with Thornby, she'd be able to see the fairy with no trouble.

"I see her," Chris said. "She's standing to the left of the trees. You have to squint a little. If you move closer, she disappears."

"I see her too," Lindsey said.

Beth felt left out. The tables had turned. Chris could see fairies, and she could not.

Chris sensed Beth's mood, having so recently experienced those same feelings himself. And perhaps tweaked by guilt for all the teasing he'd inflicted, he motioned for her to move closer.

"Come here, Beth." Chris put a hand on her shoulder. "You have to relax a bit, and don't concentrate."

Beth, Andrew, and Alex stood bunched with various expressions of squinting, mouths held just right, until one by one, they found the fairy.

"There she is." Beth pointed. "But why does she disappear when you move closer?"

"After a while you'll be able to see her from any angle," Mrs. Peasgood said. "There's a lingering enchantment in this painting, but bit by bit, you'll be able to break through."

They examined the painting a little longer, trying to view the fairy from different positions, but with no luck.

"I think we should return to the kitchen," Mrs. Peasgood said. "Beth, this might be a good time for you to seek out your fairy friend."

"The sooner the better," Beth agreed. "Chris, why don't you come with me this time?"

He smiled. Something had changed between them. He realized that he no longer thought of Beth as a little kid. Because of that, she responded to him differently.

"Hey, what happened here?" Alex entered the kitchen and pointed.

The others filed in behind him and stopped, staring in confusion.

The bottle of maple syrup, cap removed, had emptied over the table and onto a chair, continuing in thick, slow drips to the floor.

Pieces of waffle littered the table.

"Look at the pile of salt," Lindsey pointed. "And where's the salt shaker?"

A trail of waffle bits, syrup, and sticky tracks led to the open door.

"We've had visitors," Mrs. Peasgood frowned, "and you can bet they came for more than waffles."

Chapter Forty-six

Kidnapped

Bracken felt exposed. The carpeted corridor contained not one stick of furniture where they could hide. He counted three doors on the right and two on the left. Voices from the far left pinpointed the humans.

Pressing themselves against the wall, they neared the far room. Bracken eased his head around the doorframe, looking for a secure position. Nothing nearby presented itself. "We'll stay here," he whispered. "Stay alert. Be ready to run."

Inside, the humans ranged themselves around a magnificent painting. They examined it closely and then moved back to see the picture from different angles.

"I recognize the trees," Lichen said. "But what are they doing?"

"I don't know."

The dreadful boy, who had chased them earlier, stepped to the side of the painting and squinted his eyes. "I see her," he said.

Puzzled, Bracken looked more closely at the picture. His eyes widened. And his lips compressed in a frown. "Lichen, look at the painting, what do you see?"

"Trees."

"Look again."

"It's a fairy." Lichen turned to Bracken to see if he was right.

"A fairy, yes. Anything familiar about that fairy?" Bracken didn't wait. "It's Maeve," he spat. "That little traitor. Move out. We have all the information we need."

Maeve lay on her bed, her mind in turmoil. She hadn't once left the bower. Ignoring the occasional knocking at her door, she remained in her solitude. Someone again approached, and she wondered when the fairies would give up and just leave her alone.

The door crashed open, and two imps, bent at the waist, plowed through the bower. They knocked over the table and its contents, seeds raining to the floor. Maeve cried out with alarm, rolling off the bed, looking wildly for an escape.

Bracken's frame filled the doorway, Lichen bunched up behind him. "You are in league with the humans," he said, pulling through the opening, his face red with fury. "Don't try to deny it."

Maeve backed away. Her throat tightened, and her words came out in a squeak. "No, you're wrong. I've had nothing to do with humans."

Bracken looked around the room. His lip curled with satisfaction as he took in the perfectly round reflecting glass.

Her eyes darted to the mirror. "It was here, a gift from the fairies."

"Fairies are metalsmiths? I think not. Where the reflecting glass came from is of no matter. I have seen irrefutable proof, documented fact: your portrait in a human painting."

Bent at the waist, Bracken's face pinned her eye to eye. She could feel his hot breath when he spoke. "It didn't mean anything," she said, looking away, defeat in her voice. "The woman painted in the garden. I thought the painting would be better if I was in it." Her face flushed at how puffed up and vain she sounded.

"I've heard enough. You are coming with me." Bracken clamped a large hand over her mouth and backed out of the bower, dragging her with him.

Lichen appeared at the door first and jumped to the ground. "We have the fairy," he said to the waiting imps.

Bracken emerged and shifted Maeve under his arm, pinning her own arms in the process. He stuffed a leaf into her mouth. She kicked her legs, twisting in his grip. "I expect no trouble from you," he said, and meant it. Her body went limp. "Better, much better."

Mugwort hefted a saltshaker filled with syrup, careful to keep the holes facing up. Vetch balanced two large waffle squares on his head and handed a cloth bundle, with extra pieces, to Lichen. Bracken led the group, staying close to the hedge, with the hope of avoiding any fairies

Chapter Forty-seven

The Imp Court

Beth and Chris cut through the hedge bordering Mrs. Peasgood's house and their own.

"Why don't we head for the stone steps?" Chris said. "They're right in the middle of the yard."

Beth looked down the hill at the steps and the three flowerbeds she'd planted. She felt pleased with what she'd accomplished. The garden had taken a lot of work. Right now, watering the flowers was her only job. She had to use four lengths of hose, connected to an outdoor spigot, to reach them.

Chris's one chore was to mow the lawn, a big undertaking. Although made up of coarse grass and weeds, regular mowing kept it looking tidy.

Beth frowned at the roses. "With all that's happened, I forgot about the aphids."

"Don't worry, Mrs. Peasgood said you could blast them off with water."

"I know. I'll be right back." She walked up to the coiled hose and attached a pressure nozzle. Turning on the water, she dragged the lengths of hose down the hill, stopping in front of the roses. More leaves had curled and died. Some of the blooms had darkened, their petals crisping. Hordes of aphids greedily sucked the sap from the remaining healthy leaves.

She pulled back the trigger, and water smacked the aphids with a demolishing spray.

"Be sure you get under the leaves," Chris said, lifting a leaf to reveal a green cluster clinging to the underside.

"How are you going to find Thornby?" he asked, watching Beth wield the hose. "If you call out, the other things might hear you."

"Alex wants to call them boggarts."

"They're not boggarts. In the book, boggarts had long noses."

"But the drawings are made up."

"I know, but to me they aren't boggarts."

"Then call them gremlins."

"Not gremlins. Remember the movie?"

"That was made up too."

Beth tossed the hose to the ground, and they walked over to the stone steps, sitting at the bottom.

"From the description in the book, they sound like imps."

"Whatever, call them imps if you want." Beth didn't care what they were called. She fell into silence, thinking about what had happened the last few days. Her expectations of fairies and their world had been different and didn't include danger. A cavernous mouth in the water haunted her thoughts. The more she tried to push that memory aside, the more disturbing it became when it resurfaced.

She leaned over, lifting a stone and rolling it between her fingers. "Things are getting too dangerous," she said.

"What's to be scared of?" Chris shrugged. "They're just little."

She shot him a reproachful look. "What about that thing in the water?"

"Okay, that was huge. But why worry about it? It's in the water. We don't have to go back there."

"I just don't want anyone to get hurt, including me."

"It'll be fine."

"What, all of a sudden you're an expert?" she flared, hurling the stone. "You don't have a clue what will happen."

"Neither do you. I'm surprised that you aren't right into this. You're the one always reading the fantasy books."

"Those are just books. This is real."

Chris gripped her arm and finger to his lips, motioned her to keep quiet. She followed his gaze to a section of the lilac shrub, which thrashed violently.

An imp backed out of the bush, dragging a squirming fairy. He pinned the fairy under his arm and jumped to the ground where he joined his waiting companions.

Beth and Chris watched with astonishment as the imps trotted off, dragging a cloth napkin, salt shaker, waffles, and a kidnapped fairy.

"We should follow them," Chris said, leaping to his feet.

Beth rose more slowly. "Maybe we should tell Thornby what happened. I'm sure he'd know what to do."

"Unless that is Thornby. Come on. We're going to lose them." Chris took off not waiting for an answer, and Beth reluctantly followed.

With the preparations well underway, Vali took a moment from his duty as coordinator to inspect the roses.

What a shame, he thought, *the most glorious blooms in years, brought down by aphids—and so close to the celebration.* Aphids were a common occurrence with roses, but the amount of green invaders confounded him. He had never witnessed such an infestation.

Reaching up, he ran his finger along the edge of a leaf, which crumbled to powder in his hand. Brows knitted with concern, and he shook his head. Hopefully the second bush would be in better shape.

Vali intended to look, but the chatter of voices stopped him. He darted back into the shadow of the rose bush, just in time to see Beth and Chris push through the hedge. Despite all they had accomplished, Vali was not ready to meet them. He pulled deeper into the shadows and waited for them to leave.

To his surprise, they stopped directly in front of his shelter. Before he could wonder why, a deluge of water soaked him to the bone. Leaves and branches offered some protection from the spray, but not enough. The water fell in cold sheets. He hunkered down to ride out the storm.

Thankfully, the water stopped. He watched them sit down on the stone steps and listened to their conversation. They discussed the dangers of the fairy realm, and he couldn't imagine what the huge thing in the water might be. The mention of imps gave him a start.

He saw them stiffen and followed their gaze to a thrashing bush.

An imp dragged Maeve from her bower and joining three others, bolted in the direction of the woods.

Despite the shock of imp invasion, Vali was stunned when the children took off in pursuit.

Bracken's kidnapping was not well planned, and snatching Maeve in daylight risked much. Anger guided his actions, and he thought only of delivering the little traitor to the king. Ever since he had discovered her trespassing in their territory, she had been a thorn in his foot.

Usually more cautious, Bracken neglected to post an imp to cover their retreat or to scout ahead. Hoping to remain unseen, they traveled close to the hedge until they passed the birches. They plunged into the woods heading back to the meadow.

Chris and Beth came upon the meadow undetected and crouching low, watched the imps run into the tall grass.

Without pause the imps entered the meadow and, as one, threw their hairnets to the ground. Red plumes sprang to life, marking their passage.

"They've got company," Chris whispered, as a dozen more points of red joined the kidnappers. "We'll circle around the meadow and come up on the other side." His face lit with excitement.

"This isn't a game, commando boy."

"Lighten up, Beth."

North of the meadow, Chris chose a well-worn trail often used by hikers and cyclists. They passed some people out walking their dogs, and later a jogger sped by, greeting them with a nod.

The trail meandered through the woods, twisting along a steep hill. Just before reaching the top, they heard an odd sound approaching from the other side. Many voices chanted, military style and distinctly not human. Beth darted for the nearest tree, but Chris stopped her.

"Pretend you don't see them," he whispered.

With no time to question his judgment, she continued walking, avoiding eye contact as the imps crested the hill. They marched three abreast, chanting in time with their steps. Keeping her eyes trained ahead, her heart thumped, and her body braced for an attack of army imps.

Without missing a step, the imps marched around them, continuing on down the hill. When they were out of sight, Beth turned to Chris. "What just happened?"

"I figured that imps see people all the time. After all, we share the same planet. They wouldn't expect us to see them, so we wouldn't be a threat."

Beth blew out the breath she had been holding and felt her heart slow to normal.

They left the trail and moved around the western side of the meadow, keeping to the wooded area. Stepping carefully they avoided snapping twigs. The last few feet they covered on their bellies and creeping up to the grassy edge, raised their heads for a cautious look. Eyes widened with shock, unable to grasp what lay before them.

Small tents crowded a large, richly appointed pavilion, filling the entire southwest corner of the meadow. Constructed of finely woven tapestry, the central tent stepped right out of an *Arabian Nights* tale. Bright carpets lay beneath a wide canopy, serving as the entrance, and pennants waved from the central post.

A crowd gathered outside the main tent, and Beth and Chris watched with fascination as two richly dressed imps emerged from within. Their clothing danced and shimmered as they stepped from the shade of the canopy into the light. The waiting imps swept into deep bows before their monarchs, as the two stepped lightly upon a dais and seated themselves in their chairs.

From within the shadowed canopy, a movement caught Beth's eye. A salamander stretched, coming slowly to its feet. Picking its way through the crowd, it settled by the king's chair, head resting on folded legs. The sun glinted off its hide, and the king smiled, running a hand over the bronze head.

All stood in expectant silence, and from behind the tent, an imp appeared carrying the fairy under his arm. He set her on her feet and motioned two imps to take up position on either side. Walking to the dais, he bowed low.

Beth and Chris were unable to hear, but it wasn't hard to figure out what was happening. Proceedings had begun. The imp pointed at the fairy and strutted back and forth making his point like a television court lawyer. The fairy was on trial.

Chapter Forty-eight

A Walk in the Meadow

P arty's over," Chris whispered. "Watch where they take her."
An imp pushed the fairy in front of him, guiding her
through a maze of tents.

"They've got her over there, close to the woods," Beth pointed,
"the larger tent."

"I saw that too. That's good. It makes our job easier. We'll go
back through the woods the same way we came."

"I wonder who she is and why they want her." Beth looked out
at the tent city. "It doesn't look real. If we're lucky, this will just be
another dream."

"Not this time, Beth."

The king and queen returned to the main tent. Some imps
followed, but a good portion gathered outside under the canopy,
where tables and benches had been set up for the noon meal. Soon,
platters of food arrived, and the imps fell into the business of
eating.

"Let's go now." Chris said. They pulled away on their bellies
until they were well out of sight. Then they walked around,
coming close to the meadow's edge and the tent where the fairy
was held.

With the exception of one imp standing before the tent
opening, the area appeared deserted. "This is the best time to
rescue the fairy," Chris said, "while the others are eating. After they
finish, they'll be everywhere."

Beth began to shake. She wanted to help the fairy, but the
thought of all those imps turned her to jelly. Chris, on the other
hand, seemed confident that they could succeed. At this point,
following his lead was her only choice.

"How do we do this? She asked.

"Remember how the imps ignored us on the trail? I'll walk past the tent and get the imp's attention. You quietly lift the back of the tent, scoop the fairy, and put her in your shirt pocket. Casually, walk toward me. We'll take our time, maybe stop to pick a wildflower; act like we're out for a walk."

"Couldn't you come up with anything better?"

"It's the only thing I could think of, and we're running out of time. As soon as they've finished their meal, there'll be no way."

"What if they come after us?" Beth swallowed hard.

"We run. By the time they figure out what's happening, we'll have a good head start."

Chris rose from their hiding place and strode past the tent, whistling softly. The imp started in surprise. He looked back, and deciding that Chris was alone, followed him a short way into the meadow.

With no choice but to go for it, Beth willed her legs to move. She crawled to the back of the tent, praying that the imp wouldn't turn around. He had his eyes pinned on Chris, who had stopped to pick a flower. Beth drew in a breath, lifted the back of the tent, and spotted the fairy.

She sat, tied to a tent pole, a leaf shoved in her mouth. Her eyes widened when she saw Beth, who tried to smile reassuringly. As gently as she could manage, Beth removed the tent pole, and lifting the fairy, pulled the leaf from her mouth, dropping her into the shirt pocket. The tent collapsed at the back, but the front remained standing. Beth trailed after Chris, and the imp spun around to find a second human crossing the meadow.

Nothing unusual so far, he thought, watching them a moment longer. He turned, satisfied that they were leaving. *Time to look in on Maeve.* Although she was tied, she was a clever little thing, and may be up to some mischief.

He stood a moment at the tent opening, not grasping what was different, but quickly realized that the back of the tent was down. *She's wriggled loose,* he thought, forcing his way to the rear. Maeve was gone. *She must have crawled under the tent.* He ran into the woods, looking for signs of her passing, furious that she had escaped on his watch. And then he understood. *The humans. They're the ones Bracken spoke of.* He could still see them, and thankfully, they hadn't gone too far. "She's getting away!" he shouted, sounding the alarm.

Bracken sat with Mugwort at a crowded table under the canopy. "You have to admit," he said, pocketing a bite of food in his cheek, "my presentation was flawless."

"Most effective," Mugwort agreed. "What do you think will happen to her?"

"She'll get what she deserves."

"The queen holds no love for that fairy," Mugwort said.

"Nor do I." Bracken leaned forward. He plucked a boiled quail's egg from the bowl, followed by a piece of cattail bread. "Honey," he barked, and waited for the jar to travel, imp to imp, down the long table.

"She's getting away!" A voice bellowed through the camp. The imps were on their feet, benches toppled in the rush. When the king and queen swept from the tent, everyone fell in behind them. They passed the makeshift courtyard and a few outlying tents, gathering along a rise for a view of the humans.

The imp who had been assigned to guard Maeve burst through the crowd, stopping before the king and queen. "The humans took her," he croaked, bowing hastily, his face red with shame.

"Why did you let them get so far?" the king asked. "Don't tell me you didn't see them."

"Yes, I did see them, but I had no idea that Maeve was with them."

"Bracken," the king shouted.

Bracken stepped forward, glaring at the unfortunate guard. "Yes, sire."

"Their lead is too great to give chase," the king said. "You've dealt with them before, what do you suggest?"

Bracken thought a moment.

"Hurry up," the queen growled. "We can't let them walk out of here."

"Trolls," Bracken said. "They're terrified of trolls."

"Yes, trolls," the king echoed. "I understand you've used trolls before with mixed results."

Bracken saw Vetch standing behind the king, looking smug. "Well," he began.

The king cut him off with an impatient gesture. "Trolls it will have to be. How many imps will you need for a sending?"

"Just a few will produce a troll."

"No. I want many trolls, an army of trolls."

"Forty imps should be enough," Bracken said.

"Very well, choose your imps and quickly. As for the rest of you," he turned to the waiting crowd, "Divide into two groups. Run through the woods on either side of the meadow and get ahead of them. The humans are still walking. With luck we can cut them off."

Forty imps drew up into a long line. The king paced before them. "I want an army of trolls. Have them emerge from the woods, stepping in unison. The queen and I will not join in the sending." He looked at her and held out his hand. "We will watch."

Their chairs were hastily set, and the royal couple made themselves comfortable, eagerly awaiting the spectacle.

"This is far better than aphids on roses," the queen laughed.

Beth wanted to look back, but that might arouse suspicion if any imps were watching.

"Who are you? What are you doing?" A voice squeaked from her pocket.

"I'm Beth. We're here to rescue you, but it's not safe yet. We'll talk once we're out of here."

She stopped to pick a flower, at the same time, stealing a glance back at the encampment. A line of imps ranged behind them standing perfectly still.

"We've been seen, so why aren't they coming after us?"

"Just keep walking," Chris said. "Remember, they're just . . ."

"Don't you tell me they're just small. Squirrels are just small, but they bite." She didn't wait for Chris to reply and broke into a run.

Chris took a look back at the imps, and a chill crept along his spine. Turning, he charged after Beth.

"I think we're going to make it," Beth called over her shoulder. "They aren't chasing us." She plunged into the welcoming shadow of the trees, lining the meadow's edge. All they had to do now was run through the woods—about a quarter mile—and they would be home.

Chris reached the woods just behind her, and Beth slowed to let him catch up. Smiling she turned and waited, but the look of horror on Chris's face struck the air from her lungs. Looking back to the woods, a ghastly figure moved in the shadows. Then, all at once, the forest spewed hideous creatures moving toward them at a steady march. Their small eyes held no life in them, no vitality to say they were alive—just a vacant evil that pierced Beth to the heart. She backed away.

Maeve had been jostled so badly while Beth was running that she had been unable to keep her footing. Now she drew her head above the pocket to see where they were. Her face blanched as she took in the advancing host. "Trolls," she whimpered.

Beth and Chris fled back toward the waiting imps.

"No good," he shouted, grabbing her arm, "Try to reach the trail."

Movement ahead dashed their hopes as another regiment of creatures stalked from the bush.

They ran, frantically back and forth, looking for a break between the creatures. The only open area led back to the imps, and given the situation, the imps started to look good.

Beth stopped running. Folded at the waist, hands on knees, she gasped for breath. She raised her head to see Chris stumble on uneven ground, throwing his hands out to break the fall. At that, the imp queen leapt to her feet, and the king thumped his chair with excitement.

In unison, the troll's mouths unhinged, dropping like plows to scoop their prey.

Beth's heart hammered at the sight, but she grabbed his arm, as

Chris made to run. "Wait." Her chin lifted in the direction of the king and queen. "I think this is a game. They're acting like this is a sports event, and we're the other team."

The troll advance now blocked all other available exits.

"We have to take the fairy back. What choice do we have?" said Chris backing away.

"Just wait." Everything happened so fast and she knew she was missing something, but there was no time to think.

The imp king and queen jeered and shouted from their chairs, but the others stood like statues. *They're doing something,* she realized. *Is this a dream?* The troll noose pulled tighter. *They look real.* She could smell their breath, like rotting meat. Strings and scraps hung from yellowed teeth.

A burn kindled in her gut. All the fright and confusion, all the imp's tricks, gathered in the pit of her stomach. Her jaw clenched with anger. "Follow me," she snapped.

"Where are you going?"

"Into that mouth." She pointed to the nearest troll.

"No, Beth, you can't."

"Trust me, just do it." She made for the troll.

Maeve, who again had fallen into the pocket, struggled to see over the top. "Stop," she howled, "Other way, other way!"

"Follow me now." Beth disappeared into a troll's mouth.

"Beth!" Chris plunged in behind her.

Pitch black for an instant, and then the darkness wavered. Beth and Chris, still running, found themselves behind the trolls. Heads down, they pelted back to the woods. Just before diving into the shadows, they looked back to find the creatures stretched and transparent. And then, with a snap, they vanished.

Bracken cracked an eyelid, and relished the sight. *They ran like rabbits,* he thought, with satisfaction. One of the trolls wavered around the edges. Concentrating, he quickly shored up the damage. Bracken felt proud of the imps he had chosen. They had created a powerful illusion.

The queen leapt to her feet, cheering, when one of the humans stumbled. Soon she would have the fairy back, but what would she do with two humans? It had been centuries since imps had even bothered with them. *We'll have to think of something spectacular.* She thought, hooting with excitement.

The circle of trolls tightened. The only exit led straight to the imps. She sat down again, arranging her skirt, adjusting the circlet on her head, waiting for the prize.

"What's happening? They're running the wrong way!" she shrieked. Catapulting off her chair, she ran into the field, just as the children charged into the nearest troll.

A pace behind her, the king bellowed to the imps. "After them!"

The troll army vanished, and with a cry of rage, the imps poured into the field, joining the king and queen in pursuit.

Chapter Forty-nine

A Pile of Imps

Maeve abandoned her struggle to see out. Cocooned in Beth's pocket, she thought about the troll army. It was a sending, of course, but like none she'd ever seen. No fairy glamour had ever matched the magnitude of the troll encounter. Even she had been fooled, which was ridiculous. Trolls are never seen in daylight.

Angry shouts sounded, not only from behind, but from either side, spurring Beth and Chris to run faster. Their ragged breath burned in their lungs. The extra speed pulled them ahead of the flanking imps, who fell in behind.

The garden came into view, but Beth slowed, her legs heavy as lead.

"Keep going, we're almost there," Chris shouted. Beth lagged behind, and he could see the imps closing in. With an abrupt turn, he doubled back, shooting past Beth and plunging into the startled imps.

They scattered in confusion. Some, turning back, collided with those coming up from behind. Chris spun around again, and marshaling his last bit of strength, sprinted into the yard. Beth had already reached the stone steps, and Chris's heart gave a leap. He knew that he would get home.

An ugly thought occurred to him as his legs propelled him forward. *Why would the garden be a safety zone? It wouldn't. What if they attack the house?* He felt the weight of two imps clinging to each leg. One more leaped onto his back, grabbing hold of his hair. More imps swarmed on and around him. Slowly, as in a dream, he toppled.

With shrieks of triumph, more imps piled on, forming a tower of thrashing arms and legs. Hair pulling, kicking, and punching satisfied their immediate need, but the growing stack of imps hampered movement, and often they mistakenly pummeled each other.

At the bottom of the pile, Chris suffered little hurt and lay still beneath the chaos.

Beth fell to her knees beside the stone steps. She eased onto her back and lay quiet, while her thudding heart slowed. Looking down at her pocket, she watched the fairy crawl out and take a few unsteady steps.

"You're home now," Beth said.

"Thank you." The fairy hesitated a moment. "And I forgive you."

"You forgive me, for what?"

"I used to live in the truck."

Beth looked appalled and began to apologize.

The fairy held up her hand. "No need for apologies. I was wrong to be angry. You've done much for the fairies and for me. Thank you." She hopped off Beth's chest, bowed, and walked away.

Sitting up, Beth looked for Chris. She thought he had been close behind her. Not far from the birches, she spotted the imp pile. Chris's arm jutted out from underneath.

With an angry shout, she leapt to her feet and hastily searched for rocks to throw. The long hose came into view. She went straight for the pressure nozzle.

"The terms of surrender are these," the king shouted at Chris's visible hand. "You will return the fairy at once."

"And, you will swear an oath to do our bidding," the queen added, "until we decide to release you."

The king and queen leaned in closer to hear Chris's muffled reply.

Smacked by a powerful water jet, the couple lifted off their feet hitting the tangled imp pile with tremendous force. Their arms and legs splayed, and the rush of water pinned the royal couple.

Spurred on in a gleeful fury, Beth blasted the lot, and the imps bolted in all directions. She turned off the hose and waited, while Chris slowly got to his feet.

"I'm all right," he said.

The king and queen, all dignity lost, stood in shock. Soaking hair plastered their faces. Their once shimmering garments took on a pasty look and threatened to fall off like clumps of wet plaster. The king drew himself up, staring into the pressure nozzle with false bravado.

"It's not over," he said, looking up at Beth.

"Oh, but it is." Vali stepped forward, a host of fairies at his back.

The queen put her hand on the king's arm. "We're done here. We've been found out." She looked at the fairies and smiled. "It's been an exhilarating experience, and the fairy rescue, using humans, was most unexpected."

"Of course we'll be attending the celebration," The king added.

Vali inclined his head. "Indeed. You are most welcome."

Beth and Chris listened to this exchange with confusion. As the royal couple turned to leave, the king looked back at them and nodded.

Vali bowed to the children, thanking them for their help, and in an instant the fairies were gone.

"What just happened here?" Chris asked.

"I don't know. I guess the trouble is over."

"I sure didn't expect things to end quite like that," Chris said.

"I know. It feels like everything stopped in the middle of a car chase. Weird, huh?"

"Let's tell everyone at Mrs. Peasgood's what happened," Chris said.

"You tell them. I'll catch up with you later."

"Are you okay, Beth?"

"Fine, a little bit shaky is all. Go ahead."

Chris left her sitting on the stone steps and headed back to Mrs. Peasgood's house. Beth sat quietly and let the sunny afternoon calm her. The last few days had been troubling, and she hoped that things would finally return to normal—but what was normal? Since the day they'd moved in, she had not experienced normal.

Thornby sat beside her on the step, looking out on the garden. After a moment she noticed him.

"Hi, Thornby."

"Hello, Beth. You have proven yourself a true friend to the fairies. It is my pleasure to invite you to our Midsummer's Eve celebration."

"Thank you very much."

"I understand the help your brother has contributed, but you must come alone. For now, one human will be quite enough for our guests to accept. Will you come?"

Beth stood and bowed. "I am honored."

Pleased with her courtesy, Thornby also stood and bowed. "As are we. Come at dusk."

"I have a question before you leave, if you don't mind," Beth said.

"Certainly."

"Are those things imps?"

"They are."

"After everything that's happened, why are they coming to your celebration? Aren't they bad?"

Thornby smiled upon hearing the word "bad." "No, they're not bad. Mischief and mayhem are in their nature. It's what they do. Would you fault a bear for knocking down a beehive, or a rabbit for eating your vegetables? It's what they do."

Maeve returned to her bower and closed the door, uncertain of its role as a barrier. It had not kept the imps out, but she hoped the closed door would discourage curious fairies from disturbing her solitude. She doubted the imps would return, which was a big worry off her mind.

Lifting the table back in place, she gathered up the scattered nuts and dried fruit. She had enough food to hold up for weeks.

The red coverlet on the bed looked inviting. Her ordeal had been an exhausting and distressing experience. Within minutes of pulling the red velvet to her chin, she fell asleep.

Pounding on the door brought her instantly awake. She waited for the noise to stop and when it did, she settled into sleep again.

"Hiding in here is not going to help you," Juniper said, standing over her bed.

Maeve sat up in surprise, but didn't argue. "I suppose you're right, but I can't face anyone right now."

"Of course you can, Maeve. We're your family. Thornby and Vali are here, sitting at your table. Come on out and talk to us." Juniper gave her an encouraging smile.

Maeve took a seat but didn't speak, her eyes fixed on her folded hands.

"Tell us about your adventure with the imps," Thornby coaxed.

She glanced at him with a hopeful look in her eyes. He had spoken with no blaming or scolding.

Maeve took a long time to tell the story fully. When she described the crystal garden, their eyes lit with interest.

"And you say the water is heated by the fire dragons?" Vali asked. "Extraordinary."

When she completed her tale, she ended with a simple apology. "I'm sorry."

"It must have been terrible for you to be confined to your room all those weeks," Vali said.

"It was."

"I suppose it's not much different than hiding out in here, is it?"

Maeve had not considered that. "No, not much different."

"How fortunate that you had a friend like Aster," Vali continued. "Of course you have many friends here."

"You aren't angry?" Maeve asked.

"We were all reflections of a grieving garden. I never played music. Artemus chose to lounge in a greasy can instead of writing poems. You never sang. All the fairies accepted our state readily." Thornby said.

"Tomorrow, we start fresh. The celebration marks a new beginning and not just for our small area. Our guests will leave with the story of what's happened here and with hopes of renewal for their own lands." Vali gestured expansively.

"Come celebrate with us," Juniper rose from her chair and grasping Maeve's hands, pulled her to her feet. "We need you back, Maeve."

Chapter Fifty

Celebration

On the afternoon of the summer solstice, what the fairies called midsummer, Beth put in a few hours of work at the bookstore. After dusting and vacuuming, she pulled some books from the young adult section, to read up on fairy lore. There was no guarantee that what she read was true, but she found several scraps of identical information in different books. She accepted these as possible truths.

Among the information, she learned that fairies do not like iron. The color red is rare in the fairy realm and is considered to hold magic properties. Above all, it was strongly suggested that humans must not eat or drink anything from the fairy realm.

She wondered what to wear. It was a party after all, but realizing that the ground would be damp and cool after dusk, she decided on jeans, a shirt, and a sweater. She could spruce up with a necklace or colorful scarf. Should she bring her hosts a gift? Definitely.

After work, Beth visited the fabric store. Red velvet was too expensive. *I wish I had held on to that velvet dress,* she thought. She settled for some soft red corduroy instead. A bag of cotton-batting pillow stuffing caught her eye on the way up to the counter. *The fairies might like this to sleep on*, she thought. Making one more stop, she purchased several chocolate bars, before hopping on her bike and peddling home.

The moon at three-quarters full tipped the trees in silver. Stars peppered the growing dark. Beth eased out of the kitchen door, carefully closing it behind her. She carried with her a bag of gifts.

Light illuminated the trunks and lower branches of the birches. Strains of music drew her forward until she stood at the shadowed edge. Beth had imagined what the celebration might be like, envisioning a circle of fairies dancing in the moonlight. A shiver of wonder fluttered up her arms, and her eyes widened in the light of this other world.

Dancers of every size and shape whirled to the vigorous music. Drums sounded and feet tapped out the rhythm. Beth's body vibrated with the irresistible urge to fling herself into the dance. Instead she planted her feet at the edge, her heart revving with eagerness.

Pulling her attention from the dance took effort. There was much to see, and she scanned a crowd filled with unusual guests. Lanterns of soft green light, dotted the area. They hung from bushes. Some lit tables laden with food. Set at intervals, larger lights circled the dancers. Beth noticed that some of the fairies carried individual lanterns, cupped in their hands. *Fairy flashlights,* she thought.

"Welcome, Beth."

Thornby stood at her feet, smiling. He wore a purple woven vest, and his hair, adorned with leaves and berries, curled upon his shoulders.

"We have set aside an area for you to sit. From there, you can have a good view of the celebration. Because of your size, it would be best not to dance."

"I wondered about that," she said. "I wouldn't want to step on anyone."

Out of the darkness, a comet of tiny lights shimmered around them. It swooped across the grass and spiraled around Beth. She watched, astonished, as cascading sparkles moved from one direction to the next in precise turns.

Finally, hovering before her, a few light specks broke formation to land on her arms and in her hair.

"Thornby," she whispered, "what am I seeing?"

"If you were my size, you would see fairies, much like us. Our little cousins are very small."

"Can you speak to them?"

"After a fashion. Their voices appear in my mind. Fortunately, they are courteous enough to speak one at a time."

"What are they saying?"

"They have proclaimed you honored guest and welcome you to the celebration."

Beth bowed. "Thank you."

In response, all the light fairies landed on Beth, covering her from head to foot in a shimmering fairy suit. Laughing with delight, she examined her golden arm before they rocketed into the air and flew off to greet another guest.

A seat of dried grasses had been prepared for Beth just below the largest birch tree. Overhead, the leaves rustled silver, like darting fish in and out of the blue.

"I'd like to introduce you to some of the other fairies," Thornby said, once Beth had settled. "But I'm not comfortable using your true name."

"Beth is my everyday name. I have two others."

"Is that so?"

"I think my true name is when they're all strung together. When my mother calls me by all three names, usually when I've done something wrong, I feel like she definitely has the power."

"I didn't quite mean 'power' in the same sense," Thornby said.

"I know, I was joking. Most people have two or three names, some even more."

"That surprises me. I had no idea. Well then, Beth," he motioned to someone in the crowd, "there are fairies wanting to meet you."

A fairy noticed Thornby's wave and walked toward them. He wore a red, conical hat, and as he drew near, Beth saw that it was an inverted nasturtium flower.

"At last we are formally introduced," Vali said. "In all my years, which have been considerably long, I have never met a more helpful human."

"Thank you," Beth said, surprised and pleased.

"Your cooperation with the fairies has set us on the path to renewal. There is now hope that the garden will continue to recover."

"I'll do my best to help with that."

Vali inclined his head. "It has been and will continue to be a shared effort. Kindly extend our thanks to your brother and your friends for their contributions as well."

"I will."

Vali's face took on a more serious expression. "My hope is that everyone will take back news of our accomplishment here and initiate change in their own regions. Well done, Beth." He bowed and rejoined his friends.

Juniper and Artemus came by to introduce themselves and took some time to explain the different styles of dance and music.

One of the guests greeted Beth almost eye to eye. At two feet tall, she loomed large beside the gathered fairies. Her eyes, too big for her face, gleamed with merriment. Hair, the color of moss, fell in wild tangles down her back, emphasizing the quieter green of her skin.

"I represent the sprites," she said. "My name is Maj." She held out two fingers, palm up, and waited.

Guessing that this was a sprite handshake, Beth stretched out two fingers and placed them on top. "I'm Beth." As her fingers met the sprite's leathery touch, she felt the sensation of swirling leaves in an autumn wind.

A look of surprise passed over the sprite's face. "A most perceptive human," she said with approval and broke into a grin. All the while, Maj's feet moved to the rhythm of the music, tapping, stepping, and stomping. With a shrug of apology and a wink, she threw her hands into the air and spun, whirling in ever faster turns back into the dance.

After introducing her to many other unusual and marvelous beings, Thornby excused himself to join the musicians.

"Before you go, I have brought some gifts." She pointed to the bag.

"Thank you, Beth, that was thoughtful." He motioned to a group of nearby fairies, who gladly carried the bag of gifts away.

"I think you'll enjoy this next set of music," Thornby said, picking up his fiddle case.

"I'm sure I will."

The music led Beth through forests, over meadows, or running along the lakeshore. Each melody carried images and feelings, stirring her heart to laughter or tears. Her feet kept time, and her body twitched with the desire to dance. For the first time, she wished to be smaller so she could join the throngs of revelers.

Her seat afforded her an excellent view of the celebration. She saw fairies of many varieties, some winged, some not, and the tiniest specks of light swirling among the dancers. Imps, regally attired and easily spotted by their bristling red hair, danced with abandon among the fairies.

Other guests, dressed in brown, hovered by the food tables. These had long noses and rounded cheeks. It pleased Beth to see that they were particularly fond of the chocolate.

Thornby returned. In his hands he held a tiny clay cup, which he held up to Beth.

"I've read the stories, Thornby. Never eat or drink with fairies."

He smiled and nodded. "Quite right, but this is not a trick or fairy glamour. It is called 'soma,' distilled light."

Beth took a closer look. A single drop of sunshine glowed in the dark clay cup.

"Is it hot?"

"No."

"If I drink this, will I change?"

"No, . . . and yes. This is the essence of light, a single drop of clarity. For an instant, you will see yourself clearly. But that will not change who you are. What changes is your understanding. Will you accept our gift?"

Beth trusted Thornby, more than she trusted the pages of fairy tales. "Yes. Thank you."

"As you will see, you are an extraordinary human." He left her with the cup.

The music and dancers continued, but she no longer noticed them. Lifting the cup, between thumb and forefinger, she turned it onto her tongue. At first she thought she had spilled it, for no flavor or sensation could be felt.

A growing sense of peace coaxed her eyes to close. Delicious silence drew her into the depths where no thought rippled. For an instant she remained there, buoyant as in a sea. From that silence she recognized herself, not as a short, little girl, but a being of luminous beauty.

Music and laughter pulled her from that profound quiet and her thoughts returned. She tried to keep her experience from fading, but all that remained was a lingering sense of lightness and a residue of understanding.

The music stopped. The dancers pulled back forming a wide circle. Thornby stepped to the center, accompanied by Artemus.

Word circulated among the guests, "It's Artemus. Artemus will speak."

Thornby drew his bow across the strings, a single note to gather hearts and transport them into the melody. All stood silent, arrested by the sweetness of his song. When the last note faded, Artemus spoke before the rapt crowd.

"She walked the green in ages past, an opalescent silver light." Artemus turned within the circle, meeting the eyes of his audience, drawing them into his words.

"Her song ignited hearts. Connecting all to the earth rhythm, she sang of changing seasons, upheld by nature's constancy." He paused for a moment and then said, with an insistent voice, "Return the earth to it former grace, and she will walk among us. The sylvan dryad . . ."

His audience bowed in unison. As gratified as this made him feel, Artemus hadn't finished his piece. The faces in the crowd glowed. His own shadow stretched long before him. Artemus turned, eyes widening in disbelief.

She moved with the rustle of leaves, a tall glowing figure. Her arms tapered, not into hands but delicate branches. Leaves, the gold of autumn, fell in moving waves down her back. She spoke no words, but joy filled every heart.

Beth knew her as the light in the birches, had felt her warmth and her grief. *Artemus called her a sylvan dryad. She's a tree spirit.* Reaching her hand behind her, she touched the birch upon which she leaned. At that touch, the dryad turned and nodded to Beth.

The celebration had been one marvel after another, but the feeling of wholeness imparted by the dryad overwhelmed her with emotion. For a while, quiet tears slid down her cheeks until the tug of sleep pulled her head forward, and she drifted off.

Fifty-one

Out of the Pit

Beth slept. Her chin rested on her chest, and despite the chill air, she slumbered in comfort. A quick wind stirred the hair on the back of her head. Some of the finer hairs pulled sharply, followed by the solid thunk of an ax.

Her awareness burst to the surface amidst howls of pain and confusion. When she lifted her head, it came in contact with cold steel, embedded in the birch. The dryad had fallen to her knees, holding her side. A thick, clear liquid oozed through her branch-like fingers.

Intense pain, projected by the dryad, gripped everyone. On hands and knees, her side throbbing, Beth crawled away from the tree and rose unsteadily to her feet.

Evelyn Chainy yanked on the handle, struggling to dislodge the ax from the tree. Her first swing had anchored it tightly. With mounting horror, Beth saw the wiggins move in to help her. No longer shadowy figures, their solid forms gripped the ax, releasing it with ease.

Leaving Evelyn to finish off the dryad, they raced around to the spot where Beth had so recently slept. The ground cracked. Earthen lips curled apart, revealing bottomless black.

Beth stepped back. Her eyes locked on the expanding hole. Shadows, where none should be, sprawled over the lip, swelling onto the surrounding grass. Something stirred. Fingers of ice squeezed her heart, when a wiggin's hand appeared, grappling for a hold into her world.

From the corner of her eye, she saw Evelyn pull back for another blow. "No, stop," she screamed, and running inside the arc of the swinging ax, pushed against Evelyn's body.

Evelyn staggered back. Maintaining her grip on the ax, she swept Beth aside and approached the tree. Beth latched onto the handle. Not strong enough to wrench it free, she clung fiercely, hampering the swing of the ax with her weight.

With a snarl of rage, Evelyn backhanded Beth and sent her sprawling. Instead of attacking the tree, she raised the ax over Beth.

A comet of light swooped around Evelyn. She dropped the ax and swatted at the darting light fairies with hysterical cries. Beth grabbed the handle and pitched the ax into the shadows.

Hampered by the pain in her side, Beth moved slowly. Evelyn had dropped to the ground covered in a thousand sparkles. Giving her a wide berth, Beth reached out to the birch for support. From there she saw the horrors of the night unfold.

Three wiggins knelt at the side of the opening, pulling a fourth from the hole. Strega, filled with triumph, shouted instructions, pacing before the portal. With the dryad dead, he knew the hole would soon widen. A gaping orifice would spew wiggins in wave after wave. In his excitement, he hadn't noticed Evelyn's struggles beneath a blanket of light.

The dryad remained kneeling. The fairies and their guests gathered around her, doubled over, from the pain of her injury. Beth's side burned. Touching it with her hand, she expected to feel an open wound, gushing with her own blood. Her hand came away clean.

The leaking sap on the tree glistened in the moonlight. Beth moved closer to examine the cut. It gaped in an angry wedge. Sap collected on the lip. When enough had gathered, it oozed a sticky trail over the bark.

She scooped up a handful of the dried grass that had served as her pillow and stuffed it into the tree's wound. The pain in her side immediately eased. Encouraged by this, she removed her sweater. Wrapping it around the trunk, she pulled it over the cut, knotting the sleeves to hold it in place. Her pain subsided more.

The dryad rose to her feet. A soft light grew, wavering at first then igniting to a steady glow. Walking slowly, she came to rest by her beloved birch. At her feet, the portal widened. She drew herself up and rallied what energy she could.

No longer in the grip of the dryad's pain, the fairies crowded around her, lending their combined energy to hers.

Stega pulled another comrade from the blackness. At that moment the contours of the opening brightened. The emerging wiggin glowed with light, as did the eyes of the wiggin hoards below. Strega looked up into the eyes of the dryad.

She towered over him in a blinding column of light. Wiggins ran past him jumping back into the portal. As Rill started to jump, he blocked the way. "We can still win this," he said.

Rill's eyes widened with terror. The light burned his skin. "The portal is closing," he screamed. Pushing past Strega, he dove headfirst into the welcoming blackness.

Strega stood alone above the shrinking pit. Increasing light pressed upon him. The portal folded in on itself, pulling the opening closer. Soon it would leave him stranded. With a shriek of rage, he plunged into the black.

A strangled cry issued from the gold-covered Evelyn. "I did that." And then with a wail of pain, "I did that." Tears streamed, and she choked with uncontrollable sobs. The light fairies lifted, forming a roof over her head. Other fairies and their friends formed a circle around her, and the dryad turned her light onto Evelyn.

Frightened by the depth of Evelyn's crying, Beth sought out Thornby. "What's happening to her?"

"She's been released from the wiggins and is overcome with grief for the pain she's caused. At the same time, an even deeper hurt has surfaced."

Evelyn flinched from the dryad's light. Feeling undeserving of such kindness, she threw her arm over her eyes. Rolling onto her side, she pulled her legs up into a protective ball.

"I had better do something," Beth said, and she moved to stand above Evelyn. This was the girl who had come within inches of slicing off the top of her head. She could be dead right now, a bloody heap in the grass.

Beth expected to feel rage. She did not expect to feel compassion, but there it was. Her heart rolled in a wave of sympathy for the pitiable figure at her feet.

"It's okay, I'm going to help you get home," Beth offered her hand.

Chapter Fifty-two

Turning a Corner

Beth pushed through the kitchen door with Evelyn in tow. Flicking on the overhead light, she led Evelyn to the table, pulling out a chair. Sobs echoed through the house.

"Try to keep it down," Beth urged, handing her a dishtowel to cry into. "Wait here, I'll be right back."

When she opened the door to her parent's room, her father was putting on his robe. Her mother slept soundly.

"What's going on?" he asked, after pulling the bedroom door closed.

"It's a girl from school. Her name is Evelyn."

"What's she doing here?" He looked at Beth and frowned. "And why are you dressed? Where have you been?"

"She needs our help."

"Fine. But I expect an explanation later."

Evelyn's state shocked Beth's dad. Her eyes had swelled nearly shut from crying, and she didn't seem aware that he and Beth had entered the kitchen.

"We better take her home," her dad said. "Give me a minute to get dressed."

The girls sat on the backseat of the car. Muffled sobs leaked through the dishtowel.

"Where do you live, Evelyn?" Beth asked. Evelyn said nothing. Beth put her hand on Eveyln's shoulder, and asked again.

"By the school." Evelyn's voice shook. "It's the yellow house."

Beth's hand felt awkward on Evelyn's shoulder. She pulled away and looked out the window, leaving Evelyn to her tears.

They pulled up to the curb in front of a small house. "I'll take her in." She placed her hand on Evelyn's arm. "Come on, you're home now."

The unlocked door opened into a living room. By the light of a television, Beth saw a woman sleeping on the couch.

"Mom." Evelyn fell onto the sleeping form. "Mom," her voice rasped, face swollen and wet with tears.

"Evie?" The woman sat up, blinking in the blue light of the television. "Oh, Evie," she cried, gathering her daughter in her arms. "It'll be all right, honey. We're going to be all right."

Beth backed out of the door and pulled it closed. She climbed into the car next to her dad.

He put the car in gear and looking her way, lifted an eyebrow. "Spill."

"I never left the backyard. Tonight's the solstice. I went to watch the fairies dance on Midsummer's Eve."

This was not the answer her dad had expected. He looked ahead and for a moment, drove in silence. He believed her. Sneaking outside, looking for magic in the moonlight was something a child might do. Yet Beth's reply did not sound like a child. She spoke directly. Her voice held a confidence he had not heard before. *She is almost twelve,* he thought.

"What about Evelyn?"

"She just turned up. She's a very unhappy girl."

"I can see that."

She waited for judgment and sentencing, but her father said nothing. He looked ahead, watching the road. It wasn't until they turned into their driveway that he spoke.

"Beth, I don't want you sneaking out of the house at night. Think how we'd feel if we woke up and discovered you gone."

"I hadn't thought about that."

"I get why you did it. When I was your age, I sneaked out a few times myself. But it was wrong for me to do that, and it's wrong for you. I need to know where you are."

"Okay."

"We're clear?"

"We're clear."

He turned off the ignition and they got out, closing the doors as quietly as they could.

"Go up to bed and get some sleep." He kissed her on the

forehead and sent her on her way. The setting moon graced the treetops with one last kiss, before sinking below the horizon. *It is a spectacular night,* he thought.

Beth jammed a towel into her backpack and then dropped in some sandwiches, a few bottles of juice, and some cookies. "I'm going to the lake for the afternoon." She told her mother.

"Is Chris going with you?"

"No."

"Beth, I don't want you going to the beach alone."

She smiled. "I won't be alone. I asked Andrew to go with me."

"Not the celebration we expected," Thornby said to Juniper.

"I see it as a success from start to finish," she said. "The garden is clean. Flowers are growing. Best of all, we are not an endangered species."

Thornby grinned. "Did you see the look on Artemus's face? He thought we were all bowing in homage to his brilliance."

"I would have laughed, but I was too stunned by her presence." Juniper said.

"She's healing. Beth and her friends sealed up the wound this morning with some sort of poultice. Foul-smelling stuff, but I think it will do some good. Hopefully, our dryad will return for the next celebration."

"Speaking of which, I have some ideas."

"I'm sure you do, Juniper."

About the Author

Lee Rawn lives in the interior of British Columbia, Canada. Surrounded by mountains edging a huge lake, it isn't hard to retain a sense of wonder. For Lee, writing this book was a celebration of what we have and a call to maintain this jewel of a planet for the future.

Lee has written numerous short stories, is working on a second novel, and has taught workshops on many aspects of the writing process. Her love of nature spills into her other artistic endeavors, painting and pottery.

For news about her latest writing or art, visit: *leerawn.com*.

www.ingramcontent.com/pod-product-compliance
Lightning Source LLC
Chambersburg PA
CBHW061202170626
46809CB00003B/1212